Immune to Stress

Immune to Stress

By J.M. Netopier

ISBN-13: 979-8-218-91591-9

Dedication

To Angelene and Nathan

Contents

<h1 style="text-align:center">Chapter One</h1>

Angel was spreading butter on her toast, while my gaze was fixated on the TV behind her that showed explosions of Slovak villages. I lowered my head as I picked at the embroidery inside my sweater cuff, trying to distract myself from crying. I asked her to switch seats, speaking so quietly that I had to repeat myself twice before getting up to go into the bathroom. Passing the people buried in books, a student color-coding a notebook, three Pallet Ball players staring at me, I locked myself in the bathroom and sobbed, thinking about my country and my parents. How I was studying in the US, while they were bombed at the hospital. When I returned, our food settings were swapped, and Angel immediately stood up to hug me.

"I am so sorry, I had them change the TV for you." Angel stirred her coffee, a habit I knew she did when the conversation was awkward.

"It's fine. Thank you for swapping." I sat down, seeing the golden toast I left, alongside the pristinely plump grapes. Yet, Angel had gotten me a fresh cup of coffee, which I immediately grabbed to soothe myself.

"So… you submitted your PharmD application, yeah? That's exciting." Angel tried to lighten the conversation, which I acknowledged. I imagined it was hard for her, too. Having gone to the funeral last week, only to be back at Taupe University to finish her senior year.

"Yeah." I poked at my grapes with a heavy glass fork.

"Well… I'm proud of you." Angel's soft hands wrapped around mine. "Dr. Ilt would be an idiot to not accept you."

I knew Dr. Ilt, my lab mentor, had high standards and immense influence in the global immunology space. She cured malaria and created strategies to handle various viral infections. Now, she was the department head of immunology at Taupe University, the pharmacy school that complemented the two other schools in the Pallet System. A doctorate in pharmacy from Taupe meant career success and a guaranteed spot at top pharmaceutical companies like Cheshire-Yu Therapeutics, renowned for their cutting-edge portfolio of world-changing drugs. It meant that you had the chance to design your own drug or immunotherapy and to lead all aspects. Production, pricing, and which companies got to sell it. I worried my application wasn't enough, and went through multiple rounds of edits with myself, wrestling with certain word choices. I was at the level in my academics where my surgeon mother couldn't help me, the material so new that she had no idea what I was even referring to. Every year, they added one person to the doctoral cohort, and after four years, you graduated with the degree.

After we tossed our plates into the garbage vat and Angel filled her bag with various fruits, we walked from the Main Hall. A tour came out of Dorm Hall Three, the freshman hall, with a student in a lab coat. It was a myth that Taupe students wore lab coats to sleep, and I only wore mine at work every now and then. But the Pallets knew how to brand, and mandated that tour guides wear them for each tour. Indigo University students always wore safety goggles, and Harlequin University students apparently always wore a daffodil, the university flower. Even Pallet Ball, a sport unique to the three schools, mandated that tour guides wear their jerseys when giving tours to recruits. In the center of Taupe's campus stood the Neurology Building, the destination of Angel's first class. It was her major, her palace, with mine standing directly across from it. We had to part ways, since I was a teacher's assistant for a class in the Immunology Building that stood across the large pathway.

"Go get 'em, Dr. Teddy."

I watched her calmly glide through the frantic students on the stairs. She disappeared through the door that sat between two stone columns. Marvels of science occurred inside: drugs were coded and made within minutes, and research was at lightning speed. The sun reflected on the golden Neurology Building, standing across from the blue Immunology Building. I had been going to this building for the past three years. And now in my senior year, I worked as a teacher's assistant and lab assistant for the same woman.

"Good morning, class." My mentor, behind the podium in a fitted blue dress, her hair straightened and shiny, resembled a penny. She commanded the room with clarity and poise, and she put a strong emphasis on her physical appearance. Her nails were manicured and short, and she kept her hands close to her stomach as she spoke without a microphone.

"My name is Doctor Freida Ilt, and this is the first lecture of Principles of Virology. Before I begin, I will introduce myself and then allow my teacher's assistant, Tadeáš Clawik, to introduce himself." She gestured to me, casting a shadow on the projected slideshow.

Dr. Freida Ilt was the department chair of Taupe's immunology program. She oversaw the nine other labs in the department, on topics from parasites to diabetes. Dr. Ilt, like the other nine main immunology professors, had two labs: one undergraduate and doctoral lab. In her undergraduate lab, I was tasked with writing code and creating an antiviral medication for patients worldwide. Her PharmD lab, however, was far more complicated and involved manipulating viruses themselves to produce miniature factories within the body. Her lab would make viruses that increased iron in the body; others were used to increase dopamine in depression patients, and could not be transmitted. She made no attempt at diluting her work to the class, and freshmen gulped as she sped through vocabulary they would not learn until junior year. I scanned the room of eyeglasses, pen scribbling, and the occasional water bottle sip, with about 300 students who were about to be extremely humbled by the first exam.

"And now, Teddy will be my teacher's assistant. Teddy, if you don't mind..."

I stood, my legs wobbly at the sudden attention. I hated public speaking, and rehearsed my speech in my head as I stood.

"Hello everybody... I am Teddy Clawik... I am a senior here at..."

"We can't hear you!" somebody shouted from the back, which made my face warm as I walked to the microphone that stood on the podium, unused.

"Apologies, everybody. I am Teddy Clawik..."

There was a sudden, high-pitched noise that rang through the classroom, causing some people to cover their ears. I pulled away from the microphone, now double embarrassed, before returning.

"God... anyways. My name is Teddy Clawik. I am a senior studying immunology... and I am happy to be here."

A hand shot up, a boy with fluffy hair and thick glasses then stood as he asked, "Where are you from?"

"Uh... I'm from Slovakia. So, if you need me to repeat myself... because of my accent... I absolutely can." I nodded and walked to my seat as the sounds of murmurs came through the crowd. They all knew what was happening in Slovakia, and it had been a hot story for the past few weeks. Dr. Ilt, on the other hand, kept business as usual.

"Thank you, Teddy. What Teddy didn't mention was that he is one of two amazing people who work within my undergraduate lab, producing antiviral medication code. He was actually picked from this class when he was a freshman, so... it could be anybody here. Teddy, please." She motioned to the door after checking her watch. Following up the ramp, I went to the door and locked it at 9:05. Going back to my seat, I felt the same fear that I felt as a freshman. Dr. Ilt was harsh about punctuality and outlined in her syllabus that late students would not be tolerated. The sudden attention made my anxiety spike further, and I found myself picking at the embroidered cuff on the inside of my hoodie. Embroidery that I did on the flight back, to try to soothe myself for my stressful second-to-last semester at Taupe.

When the lecture ended, about a dozen students held back to ask questions. The fluffy-haired boy, whose name was Hampton, was a Pallet Ball player at Harlequin. He said he played offense, which I didn't fully understand, given that it was a three-team soccer game. I knew Pallet Ball players from Taupe would be in the class, but my face contorted into confusion, and I asked him a slew of questions about his university. I knew Harlequin University to be a media school, with other majors like real estate and marketing. He explained that while he was studying media at Harlequin, he wanted to broaden his horizons and take advantage of the Pallet Exchange program, which allowed him to stay on campus and go back and forth. His smile was sweet and cheeky, raising a mustache before saying goodbye. Admittedly, he was cute, but from what I knew about Harlequin and the fact that he was my student, I was going to refrain. I knew that the bubbly, airheaded students there would not survive Taupe's tough curriculum.

"So… what do you think?" Dr. Ilt tried to make small talk while putting documents into a folder, which happened to be resumes people had dropped off.

"They seem nice, a lot of PBall and… somebody from Harlequin," I added, standing upright.

"Yeah, that happens. Some… actually, most will drop the course. Indigo students usually stick around. They do that or switch their major if they're from Taupe, not rare. There are 306 this year. And…" She dropped a different folder of papers in front of me, with my name on a sticky note. "I would want this done as soon as you can. It's good to get into the habit of being ahead."

I frowned and nodded, knowing they were the papers due for today's class. I was hesitant to even ask for the extension because Taupe was notorious for expelling students. Except, they did not expel them, but labeled it as "Personal Misalignment to Taupe's Standards." I had watched students cry, opening the red letter in the dining hall, their so-called last supper on the blue glass plates. And I knew Dr. Ilt did not shy away from it, having witnessed a student last year beg in Dr. Ilt's office as I coded. I left the lecture hall for my next class, the one with Angel, which was in the next building over in the Neuro building. I descended the Immunology Building steps only to climb a steeper, more rugged cobblestone staircase. Since I was early, I watched students grumble out of classrooms, some puffing air from their cheeks in exhaustion, others shaking their heads. The older, more seasoned students probably had a lab to contribute to or an exam to study for. Every building had a twenty-four-hour café, and I stopped at the neurology café to get myself my third cup, alongside one for Angel. My tolerance for caffeine was so high that I was not feeling a thing and walking calmly into the lecture hall.

In the neurology lecture hall, I immediately spotted Angel's hair in the crowd of what I assumed were neurology majors in their senior year. The professor, the infamously irritating Dr. Pellin, was testing his microphone on the main stage of the auditorium that sat around four hundred people, cracking jokes to himself. Angel sat in the middle of the seats, saving me a seat with another black iced coffee. We both laughed at how we both got a refill for each other, fueling a caffeine addiction that had lasted since freshman year. I could feel stares and people looking me up and down. Taupe was silently competitive, since people wanted the top grades to appeal to pharmaceutical companies. There were always witch hunts accusing people of cheating; one even happened to me sophomore year, from a girl named Moxy Worden. No matter the major, immunology or neurology, we were all vying for spots in major pharmaceutical companies, and even though they applied to us as employers at career fairs, everybody wanted to be the best. Other universities had career centers and resume builders, Taupe students were given companies that wanted us, and if we truly wanted something different, we could apply. I had never heard of somebody getting a bad job offer or one that didn't pay at least six figures. I cracked open my notebook and wrote the date in red pen. My handwriting was small, a skill my father, a detail-obsessed financial officer, had taught me when I started school very young. The professor began to speak in a suit jacket that was way too small for his frame.

"Good morning, class. Great to see you, hope summer was restful. Mine was… well, here! My name is Nathan Pellin, and I am a lecturer and researcher here at Taupe. And, this is the fantastic class, Neuroimmunology. If that sounds like you, great; if not, the door is in the back."

He tried his hardest to make it light and jovial, but got no giggles from the crowd. For the next fifteen minutes, I almost fell asleep as he rambled about his research on mood disorders, expectations for the class, cheating policy, and attendance, but I snapped into focus when he mentioned the homework. I woke myself up with a sip of bitter coffee.

"Every week, on Thursday, there will be a five-page paper due. About anything we are learning that week. You should have submitted the paper before class, but if not, it's due tonight at midnight." I forgot to do the assignment. The slides behind him revealed a bulleted list of topics, less than half of which I had heard before. A girl raised her hand, speaking without being called on. "Material from Thursday's lecture or Friday's?" I rolled my eyes at the nasally voice, recognizing it instantly. Of course Moxy was in this class, and not that I spoke to a lot of people, but she has been wanting me to fail since day one for a reason I didn't know. Dr. Pellin blinked at her, and I was close enough to the podium to know the question irritated him.

"It's outlined in the syllabus. We cover a broad topic every week."

I watched another girl scoff, and another student shook their head as if laughing. Dr. Pellin breathed as if to move onto the next slide when the door sounded as if it were yanked open. The lecture hall door shut, echoing, before an accented voice whispered loudly, "Sorry, sorry, sorry, sorry about that." My head shot up, startled and confused. I didn't want to turn around, but there was only one person who had that voice, had an accent almost identical to mine, but slightly different. As soon as I turned around, I locked eyes with him. The traffic-light green eyes widened when he saw me, as if we weren't surrounded by almost 200 students.

"T-Bear! I didn't know you'd take this class, ahh!"

Standing in red velvet jeans and a woolen cropped sweater, he excused himself among the students in our row. I couldn't take my eyes off his hair, which was a mixture of bright red and white, looking like a peppermint. He squealed into hugging me while he sat, enveloping me in a caramel-scented cloud. When he settled down, tearing out his wired headphones from his newly pierced ears, he acted as if he was the only one in the room. Dr. Pellin stared at him like he was a clown, and Angel blinked at me quickly since she must have been equally shocked. He grabbed the black coffee with his newly painted red nails, swigging it and making a face.

"Jesus, what the fuck is this? Blah!" he said in English. Dr. Pellin seemed amused by the loud flamingo among a flock of boring pigeons.

"Well, what an exciting entrance. I guess we'll do introductions, then." Dr. Pellin cocked his head sarcastically, and my cousin clasped his hand in excitement before standing again.

"Hello everybody! My name is Cupid Czerwonovsky, and I study marketing and branding at Harlequin. I know that it seems weird to take this class when I'm at Harlequin, but I figure to take advantage of the Pallet exchange program. I am from… Slovakia, and a fun fact about me is that I'm an Aquarius! Woo!"

I could feel my eyes twitch, since introductions rarely happened at Taupe, and of course, the rules bent to Cupid. As the story goes, my father's sister, Avana Clawik, was chewing on a box of chocolates her husband got her for Valentine's Day. She was chewing a caramel cluster when the water broke, and my uncle, Stefan, rushed her to the hospital. And so, on February 19, Cupid Abraham Czerwonovsky was born. I was about two months old, my mom was nursing me when Cupid was born, and would later recount that I was being fussy that day. My father went by himself to the hospital to visit his new nephew and congratulate his sister on her bundle of joy. It was the same place my parents worked, so he knew the building well. Apparently, Cupid was such a loud crier that my father didn't need to ask which room Avana was in. Cupid and I grew up in close proximity in Slovakia, but never close as cousins beyond elementary school, due to family tensions rising at my parents' successful careers. I would see him during holidays, like Christmas and Easter, as well as random outings that fueled an illusion of a close, extended family.

Now at Taupe, I felt irritated with his rebrand so close to our parents' deaths. He looked like a clown, albeit newly renovated, captivating, and sweetly scented. Angel put her hand on my leg, sensing my irritation and teeth grinding in my efforts to stay calm. I was running on poor quality sleep, so it made it difficult to be gracious.

"Well… thank you for that, Cupid. Is there anybody else who would like to introduce themselves? We usually don't do this, I know, but… could be a good change."

Nobody raised their hand, yet I could tell Dr. Pellin was entertained slightly, thinking that Cupid was dumb. But the Cupid I knew was the opposite in his own way: he was clever, calculating, and a social butterfly. He commanded the room and demanded attention, and in return, he was easy on the eyes while entertaining with muscles, theater, and drama. He sat down next to me and smiled, revealing the pronounced canine tooth smile that he inherited from his mother. Dr. Pellin's eyes drew to me, and I was asked to introduce myself. I stood slowly, making sure that I did not spill my coffee.

"Hello everybody… my name is… um… Teddy Clawik. I'm a senior here at Taupe studying immunology. I'm also from Slovakia, from Michalovce. And um… a fun fact—"

"Is that we're cousins!" Cupid exclaimed, interrupting me and causing my face to blush in embarrassment. The class giggled, and Angel even cracked a smile at the interaction.

"Yes, we are cousins. Aside from that… um… I embroider in my free time…"

Dr. Pellin asked what I embroidered, where I held up my sweater cuff, revealing the blue, Slovak-inspired embroidery my mother taught me how to do. It was how I relieved stress the best, and I smiled at the geometric owls and flowers that grounded me on the flight back. I knew Cupid could never have the focus or dexterity for that, but his introduction seemed to overshadow mine. Angel patted me on the back while waving at Cupid in her typical friendly manner.

"Well, it's great to have… such a family affair in class. I look forward to seeing what you both will bring, given your very… different areas of expertise," Dr. Pellin continued.

I sighed, noticing Moxy glaring back at us. I wanted to send Cupid to verbally attack her, knowing that he would be like a ravenous, six-foot lion. Another facet that made me super uncomfortable about Cupid was how unpredictable he and his temper were. With that, perhaps there was some good with him being here, that maybe it could be controlled to humiliate an academic enemy. Cupid attending a Taupe class felt invasive and fueled a jealousy I have always had for him. He was taller than me and worked out much more than I did. His father was abrasive, and his mother was a gaudy purchasing agent for a weapons factory. My parents always said it took a special type of woman to name their son Cupid, but of all people, it was Avana. There was a chasm of values overall, so we barely talked to Cupid's family. Even when we did, it was tense and competitive somehow, even though our families worked in different fields, and Cupid and I had vastly different majors. Small talk was tense and slightly rehearsed, since it didn't matter how you were actually doing, but to demonstrate you were happier than Cupid's family was the goal. A small part of me smiled as the lecture started, knowing that Cupid was oblivious to the mental torture he signed up for.

The first lecture examined the chemical structures of neurotransmitters at the basic level. I could barely keep up with the rapid lecture pace, beginning to develop questions as the presentation lasted. I expected Cupid, wearing a full face of makeup, to ask me a million questions. Instead, I would look at him, watching his bright green eyes dart across the screen and take notes on his small laptop with lightning-fast typing speed. He asked well-articulated questions of Dr. Pellin, ones that were answered two slides later. Other students glared at him, including Moxy, which he seemed oblivious to. I could tell that, even though he studied at Harlequin, the laughing stock of Pallets, he had a decent grasp of Neuroimmunology. The class went over time by three minutes, and I had to say goodbye to Angel and Cupid, somewhat rushed to make sure I wasn't late to work. In a good way, it meant less time to be drained by a conversation Cupid monopolized. Saying goodbye to them reminded me of last week, watching them talk in a hushed voice in the funeral procession line.

To see Angel in the line of people, all in black and staring with sad, light colored eyes. There she was, her hair tied up in a purple ribbon, her skin contrasting with the crowd by at least six shades. In a black coat, she wore her signature butterfly earrings. The hundred or so people, most of whom were people I didn't even know, used the formal tense to talk to me in Slovak. Shaking my hands, the air misty and cold, they sadly acknowledged my losses. And then she came, and wrapped her arms around me so tightly that it was the first person in a line of people who showed me love. I remember feeling her heartbeat and her coconut perfume. The feeling of raindrops on her back. My face in her coiled hair. She hugged my cousin with a similar warmth, who stood to my right and had to crouch down. And then, as if from a magic act, she revealed red roses from her coat and placed them on the caskets of my parents. She knelt and prayed, and I remember staring at her while mechanically thanking condolences from old, Slovak military personnel. A week later, she really was an angel to me. Quiet, introverted, grounded. And the exact person I needed to get through the year.

The Immunology Building had ten floors, with each floor housing two separate wings for each lab leader. Arriving at the tenth floor, I sighed as I tapped my card and watched the metal lab doors open. I was chosen as one of her lab assistants after my freshman year, and since lab assistants were the only ones with direct access to make medical treatments, we were highly valued. There were pharmacy students who handled the drugs that lab assistants would make. There were the undergraduate lab assistants, who would produce individual or low-dose medications. I worked with flu patients, whereas the PharmD students produced far more advanced treatments for far deadlier viruses.

In the hallway to the undergraduate lab, photos of Dr. Ilt stood with various healthcare leaders. Some of the photos showed Milena Pallet, our university's president, but most showed Dr. Ilt at various lengths of her copper-colored hair over time. It was once vibrant and deep, now dulling into a softer, caramel color. Through the hallway was an opening to the undergraduate lab, with the PharmD lab's door across from it. The door had a sign that said BE BACK SOON in bright blue letters, since I knew they had September as vacation. From the small window in the door, I could see that the lights were on. The six-sided keyboard blocks, Hexboards, and the various personal items from the candidates. Preparing to see Mark at his desk, I entered the undergraduate lab. It was a small lab, with four white desks and computers alongside small machines that were the size of shoeboxes. These were the ILLUMAKE machines, biotechnology marvels that enabled users to genetically engineer and code immunology components. My desk was prepared for another day at work, with a pile of case files, a small white box of antiviral glass vials, and Dr. Ilt's signature on the top folder. I opened the box of virus vials, watching the small blue vials tremble. Holding one in my hand, I always marveled at the incredibly thin yet indestructible Pallet glass. The sparkling blue glass, the color of pen ink, with streaks of dark brown and neon green, made it captivating at every angle.

I knew the glass was specially made at Indigo University, with everything from eyeglasses, screens, windows, bottles, and plates being made at that school. My eyeglasses were made of them as well, a gift from my father before I started at Taupe. I turned on my ILLUMAKE machine, hearing Mark enter the lab behind me. We said a brief greeting, his in Polish and mine in Slovak. He was Polish American, and we could have conversations with each other not in English that were fairly fluid, given our Slavic language similarity. We didn't speak much aside from being polite, and hadn't had a class together since last fall. He was in charge of coding antivirals for measles patients, whereas I used my machine for influenza patients. With the ILLUMAKE machines, we could engineer everything from immunotherapy medication, red blood cells to bacteria, viruses to T cells. It was the first time I turned on the machine since the funeral, luckily having the last weeks of August off from my summer lab work. I could hear Dr. Ilt's voice through her office door, which was peppered with various publications from her previous doctoral cohorts. Today, I sat with the only sound of the clock ticking and began to read my coding assignment for the day. I was coding for a flu outbreak in Minnesota, and while I didn't know what Mark was working on, I could tell it was intensive by the sound of his keys. After about five minutes of reviewing a case file and typing, Dr. Ilt's door opened.

"Hello, gentlemen," Dr. Ilt continued speaking in a straightforward tone. "Apologies for the meeting. We are noticing a new virus circling around Indigo and here, but this is to be expected. Be sure to monitor your symptoms."

I nodded, understanding that there was usually some flu that went around as school started. The new students coming back from around the globe, it happens every year. Although Indigo was the smallest Pallet School, it was the densest. And, since their focus was manufacturing, health wasn't as prominent a theme compared to Taupe. Sickness here was taken extremely seriously, but a visit to the pharmacy in Main Hall meant you could get an immunotherapy specifically designed for you in a matter of days.

"Dirty glass blowers..." Mark said, under his breath, receiving a dirty look from Dr. Ilt.

"Don't say that." Tension sat in the room before she spoke again, "Anyways, there are some files on your desks today, please have them coded by midnight."

"Tonight? Like..." I was swooped right back into what Taupe was like after doing less rigorous lab work all summer. On top of that, I had to grade the papers with her hyper-detailed rubric.

"I can see what I can do," I said, with Mark and Dr. Ilt staring at me.

I tried my hardest to be respectful, but it made it hard to give Pellin's paper due at midnight, this job, and the grading that required consistent updates daily. When everybody left around 6 p.m., I luckily finished my coding work for the day, staring at the pile of papers I had to read and grade, and thought about the paper for Dr. Pellin.

As I began grading, it became clear the students had varying knowledge levels of SHV-29, the virus they had to research for the assignment. I graded fifteen papers before switching gears to the Neuroimmunology reading. It was like another language; the processes within the brain were nothing like the immune system. I imagined Cupid would never do the reading, and Angel was plugging along just fine as a neurology major. Luckily, one of the readings was on interleukins in the brain, which I moderately understood from its connection to my immunology training. Still, there were methods I had never heard of, interactions that didn't make sense. As I toiled, I got a text from Angel asking me to go to dinner. When I declined, it took thirty minutes for a pounding sound to come from the front door. I opened the lab door, my eyes strained, and looked at Angel, in pajama pants and her boyfriend's Pallet Ball hoodie, holding a plastic bag.

"I got us pasta and fruit from the dining hall, let's eat."

I huffed. "Angel…" The light above flickered, and her beaming smile radiated from her face before turning into a face of motherly concern.

"No, no. You are not spiraling with work. Absolutely not. Nourish yourself." She pushed the box on my chest, which I pushed away by reflex.

"I don't have time!" I pleaded and turned away, my eyes starting to tear. Angel quickly ushered me out of the lab.

"Teddy, we both know that if you don't eat, your cortisol is going to spike. Do you know what that does in the brain?"

I paused, going through the file cabinet of information in my head. "No…" I admitted, shamefully. Angel blinked at me awkwardly before speaking softly.

"It's the stress hormone. It was in Pellin's reading for tomorrow…"

"There's a cortisol reading?!" I exclaimed, putting my hands on my forehead.

So I was behind on grading, the paper, and suddenly behind on the Pellin readings. As I turned my back to Angel, I felt her spin me around and ground me.

"Teddy. Listen. Stop. You can look at my notes…"

"Oh, great start. First reading… and I'm already… not doing it. What's next, staring at Cupid's exam? Or…" As I stammered and spiraled quicker, Angel's eyes darted across my face like she was watching a tennis match.

I started to breathe heavily, as I felt the weight of everything pile on. It wasn't until I was sitting outside, practically dragged by Angel, that I was able to cry fully. Since she studied neurology, I often attributed that to her calm nature, her poise, and ease. I also knew her lab research focused on anxiety medication, which solidified her soothing presence as if she radiated her research. She countered my anxious demeanor and allowed me to freely voice how I was feeling. It's only been two days since I returned to Taupe, and I was already behind. Even saying it was a family emergency didn't stop Taupe or anybody here. I was forced to push ahead and relied on. With my eyes closed, I heaved a sigh as Angel rubbed the back of my jean jacket.

"Tell me how you feel," she said, gently. I looked at her holding my hands, confused.

"I just did. The million things I have…" I placed the glass container of pasta on the steps, barely touched, and steaming in the cold September air.

"No. You told me what you were thinking. Tell me how you feel." She tapped my heart with her fingers.

"I feel…" I started, only to be interrupted by her.

"In Slovak," she asserted, pulling the sleeves of her jacket down, her body shivering slightly.

"Since when do you speak it?" I shuffled in my black chinos, since my right leg was falling asleep.

I barely spoke Slovak at Taupe, and the only reasons I had to keep the language alive were dead. Nobody understood me here, and Cupid was the only person, aside from Mark, who could understand Slovak. Angel struggled to say "good morning" when she visited Bratislava, so her shrugging off the language confused me more.

"I don't. The only words I know are the swears you say when you tell me to wait, and asking if I want coffee. But… let it out. You know how to think in English, but my parents always tell me that their parents would be angry in Spanish. So… let it out."

I stammered in English before sighing and unraveling the knot in my chest in Slovak. "I am so fucking stressed and tired and exhausted and without any grace at all, I have to pull myself up. They want me… to be a machine… and… I can't tell anybody about what happened, because I don't want them to… remove me for personal reasons like they do with EVERYONE who says they are stressed. Instead, I hold it all inside. But why? Why should I? I mean, my parents were bombed, and now who do I have to impress? Who am I making proud? I feel… so lost and helpless now, like somebody… just shattered my compass of where I'm going. And now, I have to go through the motions. I have to be… thrown into this school with these… nasty students that are so fucking grade hungry… and the FUCKING grades! And the numbers, and the code. It's just… so fucking stressful. I'm just… ready to be done. I'm ready to graduate and… and… ah!!" I cried onto Angel's shoulders, shaking slightly. A group of students walked by, and I could feel the absence of Angel's hand as she was shooing them. I looked up at Angel, who wiped a tear from my face, and I snorted the mucus back into my nose. Her hands were soft and tender, gentle on my face riddled with stress acne.

"Your language is so… fiery. Even with snot out of your nose." I managed another laugh and rested my head on her jacket.

"I love you, Angel. I don't know... what I would do without you."

"I know... I love you too. I just... don't want you to be stressed, that's all. Let me know if you want the reading notes."

As I sniffled, I imagined the bacteria and viruses within my system responding to my high blood pressure. My cortisol. How my immune system was probably inflamed and irritated at me. I wondered if there was a way to stop stress on the immune system. Angel had pills and could make them in her lab, but I wondered if my expertise could be of use. I imagined what it would be like to become immune to stress. I said goodbye to Angel, thanked her for the ravioli and orange slices from the dining hall, and politely sent her off. I told her I wanted to be by myself. I knew there was no changing the circumstances, no changing the job or the papers or the classes without dropping out. Instead, I had to adapt, to mutate. I had to find a way to become stress-free. In imagining my immune system, I realized that stress was directly linked to it. And therefore, stress itself could be cured, and I could be immune.

I had never made anything that dealt with the stress hormone. I wanted to make a virus that ate the excess cortisol, and while I didn't have an exact read on my levels, I knew they were high. The fidgeting, the eye twitching, the restlessness. Angel often claimed it was the caffeine, but I knew it was stress. And besides, I had no intention of cutting coffee, so a virus would have to do. Turning on my laptop, I kept looking over my shoulder to make sure I was alone. As soon as ILLUMAKE came over my screen, I inhaled a deep breath as I'd never designed a virus before.

ILLUMAKE also had two modes: standard mode and advanced mode. While we could access both, I could only understand the standard one because of its simplicity, and my coding classes. I could use the program to produce a flu treatment based on a sample code and alter certain mechanisms. How it replicated, if it needed any other proteins from the human body. The PharmD students used characters other than the Latin alphabet, everything from Japanese characters to the Russian alphabet, to Hebrew, to Greek letters. These unique characters represented complex processes and structures that impacted how the virus behaved. That was how they could code viruses from scratch, and how I planned to try. I clicked the blue glass vial into the machine and switched the mode to advanced. I bit my nails, not knowing what to fully expect. Upon clicking around the software, I surprisingly found a simple drop-down menu and clicked the NEW VIRUS button on the computer screen. It seemed almost too simple for an advanced program. The program asked me a myriad of questions as to what the virus is used for, which called back knowledge of all of my years at Taupe. Everything from structure to replication to viral genetic material type. When I clicked that the virus was not contagious, I heard a key card ping into the lab. After my initial heart sink, I scrambled quickly and grabbed a folder from my backpack. When Dr. Ilt turned the corner, we both looked shocked at each other as I appeared to be grading a paper that did not have any marks yet.

"Teddy, what are you doing here? It's almost eleven."

"I wanted a quiet place to grade and not be surrounded by students." Dr. Ilt nodded at the lie and keyed into her office. While I heard her cabinet opening, I quickly minimized the page. She emerged seconds later and went behind my shoulder, holding a folder full of papers. It was the stacks of resumes from the previous class, the same blue folder. Was she looking for another lab assistant? I quickly moved my eyes back to her, who ended up reading the paper I was currently grading. She pointed at the center of the page after scanning it above me.

"No… this is wrong. Mark them for that." She pointed her long finger, revealing a massive scar along the palm of her left hand.

"But… the Shoedel virus is transmitted by blood, right?" I asserted, having learned it from her three years ago.

"It's vector-borne and from mosquitoes. Very different." I disagreed with her, but I didn't want to challenge her. I imagined that there was blood within the mosquito, but she would probably give me examples of viruses and how they're different, and how she's seen patients with true, blood-borne viruses.

"No half credit?" I looked up at her, seeing her hand gripping my squeaky chair.

She shook her head, seriously, "No. Never half credit. I'll leave you to it."

She glided away without a formal goodbye, the sound of her car keys and denim filling the space. She seemed slightly rushed, but I didn't need to overthink what she was up to. I opened the code again, hit continuous excess cortisol consumption, made sure the transmissibility was zero, and clicked produce. This meant that the virus would eat any extra cortisol as it appeared, which would make the person less stressed if the stress hormone was devoured. As the machine whirred, I started to write the paper for Dr. Pellin.

I submitted the worst paper of my life for Dr. Pellin at two minutes to midnight. I didn't take any sort of break before grading papers again, trying not to think about the paper I personally submitted. I know that if I were to grade it, I would fail myself. After some time, papers kept blurring until I became the database expert for all things SHV-29. Most students mentioned its excessive nosebleed trait, while others made me groan at their poorly written regurgitation of facts. I thought about quitting, both the TA job and the lab job. But, lab work made you even stronger as a candidate for pharmaceutical companies and doctoral applications to Taupe, especially because I wanted to be in Dr. Ilt's doctoral lab. I remember when I told my mother that Dr. Ilt scouted me freshman year, and she told me that it would be a lot and to make sure that the work didn't compromise my grade. Now, I was risking it all to simply manage my grades and my stress. When the light green liquid finished spinning in the machine after twenty minutes, the computer notified me of its completion. The virus, allegedly, sat in the vial, and a report showed its details. I downloaded the file and set a password for it. If I needed to know what swam in my body, at least I had the code.

I paused briefly and thought about what I was doing. There was a chance the virus would make me sick, that I would become patient zero to something awful. But, under that same logic, I could easily engineer a vaccine or antiviral to eradicate it. And if it spread, it would just mean that her lab would have more work. Once I drew the liquid, I pierced the small syringe into my arm, feeling a slight pinch with my face focused. I didn't have a Band-Aid ready, so I pressed my thumb on the small dot and fished in my bag for my first aid kit. My notebooks, highlighters, dried fruit snacks, caffeine powder packets, a wad of sticky notes, receipts, random blue thread, an embroidery needle that nearly missed my hand, and other junk. I found the small first aid kit at the bottom and placed a Band-Aid on my arm. Sitting in the chair, expecting to have an immediate reaction, I felt normal, like nothing had happened. I sat there alone in the lab, still stressed from the stack of papers I stared at. My glimmer of hope was that, as I graded more papers, I would become more immune to stress.

My heavy eyelids scanned the desk as I submitted the 300 grades, which averaged to a D. Toward the end, I did get lazy and became more lenient with the grading. I glanced at the clock and calculated that I would be getting one hour of sleep, not optimal for sitting in Dr. Ilt's class in less than three hours. Stepping outside to see the sun led to my groaning, with some muscular PBall players running on campus. I glared sleepily at them, irritated by the sound of their sneakers on the limestone. When I got into my dorm elevator, I set an alarm on my phone for 8 a.m. Dr. Ilt's class started at 9 a.m., and I needed to be alert. As I dozed, I entered a bizarre half-nightmare as my mind replayed memories.

The last time I heard my mom's voice alive was on the phone. I chopped vegetables for a salad I was going to have with Angel, while my mother was getting ready for bed. I was staying in New York for the weekend, telling my mother all about Angel's family's orange and yellow colored kitchen. The phone call lasted nine minutes and forty-seven seconds. The next morning, at 7:23 a.m., I got a call with a 421 area code. I knew immediately it was Slovakia, and I groggily yawned a formal greeting.

"Is this Tadeáš? Tadeáš Clawik?" a voice commanded. I hoisted myself on Angel's living room couch.

"Yes, this is him. Who is this?" I rubbed my eyes, registering the earliness of the call.

"My name is… General Tvec. I… There has…" I haven't woken up that quickly in my life. My hands are sweaty, rubbing against my green long-sleeve shirt. The fact that a general was calling me alarmed me and confirmed my paranoia that I had harbored for the past two years. The fear that my family wouldn't be able to defend themselves, now crystallized in my reality.

"There has been an attack…on your family. The hospital in Michalovce has…been bombed by the Russian forces. There were no survivors. I am truly sorry for your loss, Mr. Clawik."

The phrasing and pacing felt like a long sword being pulled from my stomach, dripping in warm blood. My legs felt wobbly as I stumbled to Angel's kitchen sink, where I washed the lettuce not hours ago. I threw up profusely, watching the tomatoes resurface in an awful green slop. The next few days were a blur after Angel drove me to the airport in silence, holding my hand. The customs officer narrowly missed a vicious verbal attack from Cupid, the silence we shared on the private plane from the Slovak government. The messages we received in all types of Slavic languages. Cupid's Ukrainian family members from his dad's side, distant relatives living in Prague, and Polish politicians. I insisted that Angel stay home, to which I screamed at her in one of the first furious meltdowns I had, all outside the airport.

We learned from documents waiting for us in the lavish hotel that Russia wanted more land after conquering Ukraine. Since the hospital and weapons factory were in Michalovce, in Eastern Slovakia, it was strategic for Russia, being right next to Ukraine's border. With my father as the hospital's CFO and my mother as a surgeon, the hospital was bombed shortly after the weapons factory where Cupid's parents worked. Luckily, foreign aid helped to push Russia back, but it was too late at that point. My parents were dead. Cupid's parents were dead.

Constructing the photo wall was the most draining part of the trip, given that we only had one board to use and had to decide which photos to display to the world. We sifted through all of the photos on the floor, with a case of beer and smoking cigarettes. I put a picture of my mom and me in our kitchen on the board. I was no older than two, with berry jam all over my face, in a wooden highchair, and my mom was giving me a confused look. There was one photo that, when I saw it, made my face curl up and cry. I sat on the floor, next to Cupid, who held me as I whimpered with a photo of my father and me at my very first research presentation at Taupe. My father and I had the exact same face, except I had my mother's narrow eyes and smile. He stood with his thin metal glasses and brown suit, with my smile beaming as I presented my progress update of my first flu season working with Dr. Ilt. I woke up thinking about that project and my father, staring at the memory box in the corner of my dorm.

I knew that it housed sacred memories, ones that I could not stomach to unpack. I knew I was too fragile to open them and knew that I would when I could.

Chapter Two

It was about two weeks after injecting myself that the banality of Taupe settled in. The boring food, the lack of social life, only Angel and I watching reality TV saved our boredom. Every so often, I checked the virus file to make sure that it was, in fact, unable to be transmitted. Each cough I heard in lectures, every sneeze, I would find myself worried that my experiment was spreading. The experiment that, unsurprisingly, failed. I was still stressed, still had work that seemed to overwhelm me. It created horrible sleeping patterns and led to numerous grading errors that were easily fixable. The only glimmer of rest was spending the weekends sleeping and cleaning, if not sewing. One Thursday, Dr. Ilt stood in the doorway and addressed Mark and me sternly. Even though it's been almost three years since my first day, her standing in the doorway always brought anxiety within me, like she would expel me for any reason.

"Would you two mind… coming into my office?"

Mark and I didn't look at each other but rose obediently. With the weather suddenly becoming colder, Mark's heavy wool sweater brushed up against me as we passed the empty desks. Upon navigating to the modern, purple and gray seats across from her glass desk, Dr. Ilt inhaled before speaking, holding a glass mug of steaming black coffee.

"We are noticing… a bizarre phenomenon here at Taupe. We have a student who is presenting… odd symptoms of what we suspect is a viral infection, although not confirmed. She's currently being quarantined."

Anxiety rippled in my chest when she said viral infection. My eyes shifted across her forehead wrinkles, landing on her cold blue eyes that were intensely staring back at me. Mark cleared his throat before speaking curiously.

"All right… so, we're developing an antiviral for her?" It seemed obvious to state, but debriefs like this rarely happened. Even though Mark was hired a year after me, meetings with the three of us were rare and would happen in the conference room next to her office. Dr. Ilt's tone reflected that, as if her massive office that overlooked the campus was too cramped for the three of us.

"Yes, but… it's more complicated than that. This isn't a flu virus or measles. It's unlike what we've seen. The patient's sclera… the whites of her eyes aren't white. They're green, sometimes blue. It looks like a bruise."

Dr. Ilt seemed concerned and scared, something that was unsettling to see. And, in my years at Taupe and countless virology classes, green sclera was something I had never heard of. Jaundice made eyes yellow, but green and blue were alien to all of us.

"That's… how does that even work? The whites of her eyes are bruised?" Mark seemed equally puzzled.

"It looks like that, yes. So, each of you will receive a vial of her blood. Please use masks and gloves when—"

"When handling sensitive biohazard material, absolutely," Mark finished her sentence, which she responded to with a nod and by standing.

"Yes, well… I will get those to your desk; they're in storage right now. But, in the meantime, review the file. When you have the sample, tell me what you find. Any… biomarkers or clues as to what this could be, or how to treat it."

Dr. Ilt handed us each a standard case file folder, approximately fifteen pages. We both got up, Mark already scanning the folder as he moved slowly past the gray couch and glass coffee table. When we got to our desks, I opened the file and read the infection overview.

"Oh, and gentlemen? Your work on this will be considered in your doctoral application," Dr. Ilt spoke in front of the metal doors, and when they slammed, Mark and I looked at each other.

I gasped when I opened the case file, revealing the patient was Moxy Worden, the girl I hated. Her student photo, with the same beige background all Taupe students had, showed her smiling innocently in her freshman year. She wore her black hair in a ponytail and a polka-dotted shirt the color of a canary. She was born on November 17 and was from Chicago. I knew she was an immunology major, but I didn't know that she worked with Dr. Alten, who produced antibiotics a floor below us. It confused me as to why I never saw Moxy at all. Now, she was afflicted with a virus that turned her eyes green.

As Dr. Ilt handed me the blood vial with plastic gloves, I immediately knew what I was going to do. I had to see if Moxy had the virus I coded. I couldn't imagine being responsible for this, and even though she falsely accused me of cheating, that she exemplified everything wrong with Taupe and the medical education system as a whole; it would be cruel to infect her. Clicking her blood vial in the back of the machine with a slight tremble, I ran the analysis quickly on her blood in a matter of seconds. She had normal vitamins and nutrients, except for low vitamin D, and her white blood cells indicated she was infected with something.

I darted my head around the lab, seeing Mark crouched in front of his monitor and reading while Dr. Ilt's door was closed. I opened my designed virus file, after putting in the password, which was my father's birthday, a cascade of random code sprawled on my screen. Right now, it was in advanced mode, but I needed to convert it to something I could understand and read. I converted it back to standard mode, and upon doing so, I was able to get a sequence of my virus. A set of numbers and letters that was unique to what I designed. I heaved a deep breath before searching Moxy's blood for the presence of virus 38FV29H397Q.

"This shit is so fucking hard," Mark said to me in Polish.

"Yeah… I know her, though, so I want to help her."

It was a half lie, I didn't care about Moxy until now, but she could be used as a stepping stone for my career, a chance to show up Mark, and add to my doctoral application. In Moxy's blood, I found a list of all the viruses that currently infected her. I knew that most of them were useless, just swimming around her system and not presenting any problems. When I entered the code for my virus, slowly plucking the letters one by one, I hit enter and watched the screen load. After ten seconds, my eyes widened as the exact letters stared back at me.

Moxy was infected with my stress virus.

I closed the program as calmly as I could and went to the bathroom on the ninth floor. I walked past Dr. Alten's lab, seeing a similar computer lab set up through the large window. I passed by students in lab coats, some scrolling on the Pallet Portal social media page. It was the main way we got Pallet news, and kept up with other students from the other universities. I couldn't think about the other universities now, and pushed into a bathroom stall seconds before I threw up. Once I flushed, I looked in the mirror while scrubbing my hands quickly. My own sclera were white, surrounding my moss green eyes that were glassy. What scared me the most was hypothesizing the chain of contact, exactly how she got the virus. I didn't talk to her, which meant that she got it from either being in Pellin's lecture with me or by coming into contact with somebody I knew. Both were unsettling and meant that this virus was far more worrisome than I imagined. For the entire day, I sat with my mind racing on what to do. Do I admit that I did it? That I infected Moxy, and who knows how many others? That I tried my best to be stress-free and only infect myself, but only to infect other students by accident.

Something dawned on me.

I had the code and had the virus synthesized. I knew that Mark didn't, and I could find a way to use that to make myself look good. It wasn't a competition, per se, but looking good in the eyes of Dr. Ilt in any way added to my application to her doctoral cohort. I drafted a bulleted list of talking points about my virus, being sure to reveal just enough information to appear brilliant and not the source. When, at 5:30, we were called back into her office for updates, Mark and I stood at opposite ends of her desk.

"What were you able to find?" Dr. Ilt's office was decorated with more photos of her, more certificates that intimidated me. As Mark spoke, it settled how much influence she had over my career.

"Well, her cell counts show that it's definitely a viral infection. So, I dug through her code and have a list of 500 viruses that I think it is. All of them produce some sort of output, but I'm uncertain if they are sclera pigments. I went through their coding, but it was tricky." I had thought about getting a description of the virus or the others on my list. I was afraid that revealing too much or seeming too smart about it would give it away, a worry that Mark didn't seem to have as he impressed Dr. Ilt.

"Hm, interesting. Teddy?" Dr. Ilt turned to me, the sun going behind the tall pine trees that circled the campus.

"I think I have the virus… I mean, I found the virus that's causing the green eyes." I started to get intriguing reactions from both.

"Is that so? Tell us more." Mark scoffed lightly while Dr. Ilt spoke with her arms crossed.

"It's… 38FV29H397Q," I slowly said all the letters and handed Dr. Ilt the paper I printed, leaving Mark to watch skeptically.

"And, tell us, how did you decide this was the one?" she said, focused.

"Well… Moxy has trillions of viruses in her system. And, when you rule out the viruses we have in the database… ones that we have seen before… you get around fifteen. I agree with Mark, her counts show it's definitely viral. But this is a simpler group to choose from. Maybe there's overlap with Mark's list."

"That's a great point, but… why this one? It could have been one of those trillions you cast off."

"Yes, that's true. This is just my estimated guess. I think it's 38FV29H397Q, or at least one of those fifteen."

"Well… it's a start. I'll have Peter take a look at them and send me the full list. Mark, send what you have as well."

I knew she was talking about Peter Cheshire-Yu, a Taupe alum who invented the machines and software we use. I remained composed, solidified in the well-constructed lie. Dr. Ilt dismissed Mark, leaving me alone with her. She stood, looking behind her window to the Pallet Ball stadium and Khill Library. They were two sides of Taupe, the academic and athletic, all under the watch of her.

"That was impressive, Teddy. Great thinking." Her words produced a slight smile on my face, and I thanked her before leaving.

"I was always impressed by your… savviness, your ability to think through problems."

"Thank you, I got it from my mother… in Slovakia." That level of vulnerability felt unnatural, but from the ego boost she had given me, I felt obligated to share.

"Well"—she walked over to the door, opening it and gesturing out—"she must be very proud of you."

I forced a smile and approached my desk, swallowing any emotion I had. I could feel Mark glancing at me every so often. I didn't want to talk, since I academically steamrolled him. The dynamic now shifted from coworkers to competition, and he left me in the lab without saying goodbye. I would probably see him tomorrow, since it was the first career fair at Taupe.

The next morning, after rinsing off the night sweat, I combed my hair to the side, with cheap hair gel I would save for special occasions, my fingernail feeling the bottom of the tin. I pulled down my eyes and blinked some eye drops in, yawning in the process. After two hours of sleep from doing readings and submitting grades for the second virology assignment, I splashed cold water on my face and slicked my hair back. I stood slouched over my bathroom sink, loopy, nauseous yet hungry.

I came back into my room in a towel, pouring coffee into a mug while I yawned again. I had nothing to eat, but assured myself that coffee alone could fuel my morning. Angel bought me ground coffee as a small gift, and I constantly thanked my mom for the coffee machine I had at Taupe. My mom said she lived off coffee in medical school and used the machine every day. I thought about what my mother was like in medical school and the copious amounts of coffee she drank.

On the walk to the Main Hall, I sent the virology students a message regarding my office hours tonight. They could review the grades for the first two papers and ask any questions they had. I would be at the Khill Library at 8 p.m., and although it was a Friday, I knew students would attend. It was my first office hours, and I imagined it wouldn't be that hard, but what worried me was the tenacious, number-hungry students.

The Main Hall buzzed with people in suits and their rendition of nice clothing. I tugged at my gray suit leg, which happened to be short in the legs, the same suit I purchased freshman year. Like a lighthouse, Cupid towered in a white, iridescent suit. He locked eyes with me, sporting some intricate white eyeliner, the crowd parting ways at his confident presence.

"What are you doing here? It's for Taupe students…" I asked coldly.

"Well, good morning to you, too! I wanted to see what was going on, and Dr. Pellin told me about it at office hours."

His energy and jovial nature got underneath my skin, and I hoped that he would be denied. A woman with a briefcase came up to Cupid and complimented his shoes, and my head tilted down as I registered the peach colored stilettos, some sort of colored reptilian skin that glistened. Compared to my scuffed, opaque oxfords, he looked far more captivating. We separated, and with no sign of Mark or Angel, I walked in alone. I watched the horde of students flock to their assigned seats.

The auditorium, which was usually dedicated to studying with long tables, seemingly transformed into rows of individual tables and two chairs. It was employer speed dating, and why students went through lengths to attend Taupe. The students didn't apply for jobs; they applied for us. I had no idea what to expect; all I knew was that you would sit down and speak with the people on your list who wanted to speak with you. I found my seat, my full name, alongside a notepad, a red pen, bottled water, and a folder. I slouched in the chair made of metal, and I was relieved when Cupid was not next to me. I read the list of nine job offers, excited about the final company on the list. After ten minutes of leg bouncing and glancing around the room, the person at the top of the list was the first person to arrive, and did so charismatically.

"You must be Tadeáš!" Her accent was southern, and she completely butchered my name. Her fake teeth gnawed on gum like a cow, and it took my eyes a second to truly scan her tanned face.

"I am Alexa Parfin, talent acquisition at Zygod Labs."

I nodded, but I had never heard of them. I listened politely as she told me all the drugs they made, their focus on cancer, and their locations, including right here in Hartford. When I didn't have any questions, her demeanor changed visibly. I had rejected the job offer, so it seemed. She walked away shaking my hand, and I could tell she was offended. I was apathetic toward every company except the last one. More representatives came and went, dropping off formal offer letters, pamphlets, business cards, and other branded items I would throw out. There was Joan Silva, who discussed all the benefits of working with an insurance agency. There was Ameer Gillon, who worked in fungal infection treatments, impressed by my work with Dr. Ilt.

With the event coming to a close, I stared at my blue watch face when a figure materialized, leaving the best for last. I shot my head up and cleared my throat, expecting to see Felicity Del from Cheshire-Yu Therapeutics. Yet, my jaw dropped when there was no woman in front of me, but Peter Cheshire-Yu himself.

"Is this seat taken?" he asked, smiling.

He had a round yet young face, and smoothed his black suit jacket as he sat. "God, they haven't changed these chairs, have they? Same ones from when I was here." He cleaned his sleek glasses using a cloth from his pocket.

I smiled in amusement, but my heart rippled in anxiety.

"So, Teddy…I understand you work with Dr. Ilt. My team is looking at the list you sent. Tell me about that."

The energy of the event was completely flipped now, since I felt like I was being interviewed. Yet, I was eager to brag about myself to him. Dr. Cheshire-Yu's lab could prevent pandemics, counteract bioterrorism across the world, and was seen as the top research facility for immunology. The United States government leaned on them, as well as other international bodies.

"Aside from this… one patient, I work with localized flu outbreaks. Receiving viral code, deciphering how it will play out based on how the virus is wired. Over the years, I've helped communities around the world, right now I'm working on a case in Minnesota, an affected daycare."

"What was the largest number of people you've served with your treatments?" He seemed to take notes on a small notepad.

"I believe around fifty."

"Impressive. Certainly room to grow." His posture radiated confidence before asking another question. In the corner of my eye, a student loudly joined hands with an employer, likely getting an offer he wanted. I was in the process of doing exactly that until Dr. Cheshire-Yu asked a question I didn't understand.

"I'm assuming you code on six?"

It threw me off, not expecting a coding question of any kind. "Pardon?"

"You code on a six-sided keyboard, the Hexboard?"

"Oh, um…"

I didn't code on a Hexboard; I was only coding on the flat keyboard. Dr. Cheshire-Yu figured out how to code not just in the Latin alphabet, but to manipulate the Greek, Cyrillic, Hebrew, Chinese, Arabic, and Braille alphabets to be used in genetic coding. He found out that DNA wasn't just A to T and G to C, but it was far more complicated than that, and that strings of all those letters could be used together. The problem was that only doctoral students used Hexboards.

"No, I… I used only one-sided keyboards."

His black eyebrows heightened, and I could tell he had to repaint the image of me in his head with that new piece of information. "But, you… what? You're not a PharmD student?"

"No, I'm a senior."

"Oh… you could have fooled me! Dr. Ilt praised you and your intellect, and that list seemed thorough. She said you pretty much found a virus based on symptoms. I just assumed you were graduating with your PharmD." I didn't know whether to smile or be concerned, since the conversation could go either way.

"No, I think they are on vacation," I reminded him.

"Oh! You're right, it's September, yup. Well, anyways…" As he rose, I felt my heart sink as he handed me a gold business card. I wanted to pull his arm down back to the chair, tell him I lied, and that I was a PharmD student.

"Reach out when you complete your doctorate. I'd love to chat."

Watching him walk away made my demeanor change into a hollow bitterness. The opportunity I wanted seemed to walk away, right in front of me. My hands felt clammy, and my throat tightened, as I watched one student shake someone's hand ecstatically. I was somewhat happy that Peter Cheshire-Yu was last. If he were first, I would have sat with my arms crossed as somebody gave me a stress ball while talking. I should have lied, told him I was a PharmD student. But any question regarding the advanced coding methods would have unearthed the truth quickly.

Once I was finished with self-loathing, I dug my nails into a stress ball, suddenly extremely hungry. I looked up from my phone, checking the dining hall line wait time, to see Mark relatively close to me. I waved at him awkwardly and, not knowing how to act, but I could tell from the look on his pale face that something was wrong.

"Hey… everything okay?" I said in a hushed tone.

"Yeah… I… um… I didn't get an offer. Nobody showed up." His brown eyes were shifting around the room, as if he was looking for somebody anxiously.

"Is that normal?"

He was shaking his head and looked at my eyes. His irises were normal and light brown, but the whites appeared to be a light shade of blue. It must have been his blue suit, yet it threw me off guard, given Moxy's case. I didn't want to concern him further and tried to reassure him. Besides, how could I tell him that his sclera was blue?

"Um… hey, I'm sure that there was a mistake or… you know… there's always other fairs. They happen like… every month, right? So just do the next one."

I struggled to comfort him, given the lack of interaction we had. It was ironic, since we spent the summer seeing each other every day. When I put my hand on his shoulder and assured him gently, his anxiety visibly softened a little.

"Yeah… you're right. It's the beginning of the year, that makes me feel… so much better. Thanks, man."

He patted me on the shoulder like I was his friend, and walked away slowly and without urgency.

In that moment, there was some strange camaraderie I felt between us. We'd worked together now for over a year, and given Taupe's social landscape, one might even call him a friend. As the sun went behind the clouds, the auditorium became a dim gray as people started to funnel out.

After grabbing lunch at the extremely full dining hall and taking a long nap, I made my way to the Khill Library to answer questions about my grading. I swung open the tall, dark wooden door with the noise echoing through the long study floor. The Pallets converted an entire cathedral into a library: confessional booths into intimate study rooms, pews into desks. Stained Pallet glass sparkled blue, green, and amber light on the ground, past the portraits of the Pallets and other leaders. I decided to choose the confessional booth that was the largest, under Angel's lab leader, Dr. Francesca Briar. The sun was positioned so that a large streak of blue plastered over her eyes, looking like a mask.

Once I got settled, I twisted my back to see if Angel was organizing books at the main desk. As if she waited for me to notice her, she waved at me to come over. She was wearing one of my favorite sweatshirts, a printed pig wearing a crown in a pink dress.

"Here we are, yet again," Angel said with a sigh while I was tapping my fingers on the dark wooden help desk.

"Keeping these kids motivated," I joked.

"Something like that… oh, what the hell." Angel revealed a textbook that had at least twenty pages ripped out of it. I chuckled, knowing that this was not the first time this had happened in the library.

"Are people that… petty to try and get good grades? The companies literally apply for us." Angel shook her head while writing some sort of report, writing down the ISBN number.

"Yeah, it was some shit Moxy would do."

Under normal circumstances, I wouldn't feel bad. But thinking that she was in some sort of hospital somewhere, terrified and with green sclera, I felt guilty. Yet, Angel laughed.

"Oh, how was the career fair for you? I got two offers." I high-fived her before telling her about my job offers and how Peter Cheshire-Yu thought I was a doctoral student.

"I mean, that's a huge compliment coming from… oh, is that your stuff? Somebody's there."

I turned around to see somebody standing awkwardly outside the pew. I sighed and wished Angel goodbye, since now my job as a TA resumed, and I had to be an expert now.

The table couldn't hold more than two laptops and coffee cups, with the old wooden wall forcing good posture. His name was Marcus, and once I found his paper, I awkwardly revealed a failing grade. I explained how he didn't go in depth on why the viruses behaved the way they did, and emphasized that he needed to discuss diagnosing the viral infection. I could tell he was a freshman based on his concern, but I assured him that it was one paper, and it wouldn't hurt him. When he left, he gave me an awkward hug over the table that flooded my nose with cologne. The second person arrived five minutes later and gave a huge smile as he approached.

"Teddy… how's it going?" Paul, Angel's boyfriend, said as he took off his backpack. He ducked his head below the arch of the booth, narrowly scraping his head.

I had to hand it to Angel; her taste in men was incredible. He spoke with the most gorgeous lips and teeth, and his twisted hair made his face look even sharper. But, I did end up failing his paper, which was met with him dramatically wincing at the score.

"I thought you were my friend…" he said, half joking.

"No, I am, absolutely. I just… I have a job. Like you have a PBall game… would you miss a goal for me?" I pointed out, which seemed to get the point across. I have never seen a single game, but I knew the basic rules about the three-team soccer game.

He weighed both options before concluding, "Well… you got me there."

"So… let me see… oh, yeah, all right. Your problem was you didn't cite anything. You just… talked."

It was no wonder the Pallet Ball players got a general pharmacy degree, taking only entry-level classes in both schools. There were some Pallet Ball players who did single, focused majors. Given their practice schedule, those were the people I was worried about in the employer recruitment process. Paul was not one of them and kept asking extremely dumb questions.

"Isn't that what you wanted?" His puzzled tone almost made me laugh, but I was in a professional mood and did not want to cruelly laugh at his failed paper.

"We want more researched, thorough papers," I explained, gently. I felt like my mother explaining biology to me when I was a child.

"I know it's tough, but… here, let me write a plan… how to…" I asked him about his time commitment, and found a relatively cohesive homework plan that worked around his morning, late morning, afternoon, and night practices.

Once finished and the back of the paper covered in a bulleted list of expectations, another person emerged and waited for their turn. It was a girl with forehead acne and the brightest blue eyes that pierced me before she sat down. As I explained how the virus was transmitted, I was shocked to watch her eyes become full of tears. Then, like clouds rolling in, the whites of her eyes turned a dark plum. My eyes widened in shock as she rambled about how confused she was, but I didn't want to stress her more.

"And like… this is really important because… Dr. Ilt studied this thing, and I really want her to like me and… I mean, a lab position with her would totally…"

"Connie. Listen." I brushed my hand on her fidgeting, bandaged hand. Feeling how warm it was almost made me recoil.

"Dr. Ilt isn't that brutal. Yes, she's harsh and… has high expectations. But, you're at such an amazing school already, please don't… bully yourself into getting a lab position."

I watched with every blink of her eye. As I explained that, they became white again. I released her wrist and watched her heave a sigh of relief, nervously smiling as I handed her the failed paper.

It was around 11 p.m. when I stood and packed my things. Tossing the empty energy drink (which Angel dropped off between students), I sighed, putting on my denim jacket.

"Teddy?" a voice called, behind me and slightly high-pitched.

"Oh, my office hours are…" I turned around expecting to see a student, but was instead confronted with Moxy staring back at me, with a face mask.

"Oh my… Moxy… hi. How are you feeling?" Her eyes seemed normal, and I became acutely aware of her physical appearance for signs of sickness. Her hair was greasy, her skin

"I'm better, thank you. I was told that you helped… isolate the virus. Dr. Ilt visited me and the other student, I mean, through a glass window."

"The other student?" I blurted out.

"Yeah, they were a Pallet Ball player and reported blue eyes.

"So… why are you… here?"

"I just wanted to ask… do you know anything about it? I've heard people talk… at the pharmacy. People are saying it's some sort of leak, and I knew you worked with her."

"We… we don't know a lot. We made some antivirals, your antivirals. I'm just glad it worked."

"Moxy…" I smoothed my hair, both irritated and tired from all the virus conversations I'd been having. As for gossip, I didn't have time for it, let alone from Moxy Worden, who accused me of cheating in Dr. Moody's Infectious Disease Epidemiology class.

"Why are you telling me this?"

"I want… to know if you know… look." She sighed, while my eyes fixated on her nervous tics, her seemingly disorganized way of speaking.

"I know that we don't like each other, okay? I work at the pharmacy, you got her lab spot. But, whatever. But, this virus is starting to go around, I swear I've seen some people asking for… treatments for it. People are saying Dr. Ilt did this. Or, the Pallets did. I don't know, but this bug came out of nowhere, and people are getting it. I just… wanted to see if you knew anything."

I registered Moxy's paranoia, her self-preservation. It was difficult not to have my face twist, reacting to the conspiracy theory. I told her I didn't know and lied about having somewhere to be, which was my gray colored dorm room with a TV show on my laptop. I left quickly. Angel was replaced behind the desk by a tall boy in glasses, whom I awkwardly waved at, thinking it was her.

Chapter Three

I descended the steps before the dining hall entrance in Main Hall and knew there wouldn't be a line since it was around seven on a Thursday. There was a Pallet Ball player in front of me who got their vial of medication quickly. I overheard it was some sort of antibiotics, and smiled politely at them as they walked by. I wondered if I would see Moxy or anybody else I knew working. I stepped up to the tall, muscular pharmacist with a buzz cut.

"Hi, my name is Tadeáš Clawik, picking up for…"

"Student ID?" I recounted the nine digits, which he clacked into and looked up.

"The… uzkozatine. Yeah, it's in the back."

As he scanned my anti-anxiety medication I started freshman year, I looked at his computer screen again.

"You're… on the Silva plan? The student one?"

"Yes. Should be all there."

"Oh, it is, yeah. Do you want to have your reading? Your last one was… last year."

"No, uh… that's okay. Actually, sure."

"All right. I'll just take you over here." He walked me over to another booth while he held out his blue-gloved hand.

"Small prick, and we run your vitals and everything. You know the drill." He gestured to the ILLUMAKE machine, one that accessed personalized vitamins, antibiotics, antivirals, and even led me to anti-anxiety medication my freshman year. But now, I had the ability to test my own blood, and it made little sense for the pharmacy to test me. I could see my counts, and didn't want some pharmacy worker reading my levels. And, at worst, seeing that I was positive for the stress virus. I politely declined, stating that I had a study group I was leading. He nodded and sighed, turning off the machine and taking the next client behind me. I glanced at their sclera, noticing that they were slightly purple.

It had been about a week since I saw Moxy, and conversations surrounding the now labeled "Bruise Eye Virus" had emerged. Angel and I talked about it over breakfast, and it was briefly mentioned in Dr. Ilt's class. She even instructed me to send a Portal message to students that colored sclera would mean to stay home from class. She made sure to attach campus resources, and at work, we kept receiving patients with BEV. After Peter Cheshire-Yu confirmed I was correct with the virus, mine and Mark's work was no longer about measles or the flu, but all centered around BEV cases at Taupe. Every day, I wondered whether or not it was spreading around the world, the true power of my virus.

"Hello, you two. Come to my office, please." Almost in unison, Mark and I closed our computers and looked at each other as we entered Dr. Ilt's office. The rain outside painted her windows, with the overhead light providing a gross contrast. Inside sat Milena Pallet, in a black suit with noticeably large Pallet glass earrings.

"Hello, wonderful to see you both." She sat on one of Dr. Ilt's couches, adjusting a bright purple cylindrical pillow under her arms before gesturing to the couch across from her. "Please, have a seat."

Having a closer look at her, I noticed that Milena's eyes, behind the silver glasses, were different colors. Her left eye was a dark hazel, and the right one was an even darker blue. Dr. Ilt sat down next to her, crossing her legs and smiling. She didn't need to introduce herself, and I had the feeling she had heard enough about us.

"Well, it has come to our attention that one of the members of Dr. Ilt's doctoral cohort has dropped. The first year." Milena's tone was flat, and I had no idea where the conversation was going. Were they sick? What happened to them?

"Now, normally, it takes us a year to go through applications from Taupe and other universities. But, given the circumstances, we have decided to accept one Taupe applicant for immediate acceptance." Milena cleaned her glasses with a tiny cloth, with Dr. Ilt contributing to the conversation from her desk.

"It's only fair, since the person who… left the cohort was from Taupe."

I couldn't quite figure out why, but the conversation didn't feel right. They were hiding something, even though the framing seemed relatively neutral. A crack of thunder was heard outside, which caused Mark to jolt slightly.

"We wanted to tell you that you two are the finalists." Milena nodded, slowly revealing a polite smile.

What? It seemed too good to be true. Mark pumped his fist before returning to professional reality. I smiled before sensing that there was a caveat.

"Well, once again, you two had better… applications than around 850 others. That being said, we need your help. Specifically, with Indigo."

"Indigo? Like… the engineering school? Is there something wrong?" I asked, confused by the sudden shift.

Milena's tone was matter-of-fact, and it was obvious she had decades of business experience. "The manufacturing school, yes. They are having an outbreak and…

"We need you to… well, to guide us. We, luckily, have gotten the complete viral genetic material from your work and observations, with Peter confirming it. We think it is linked to stress somehow," Milena admitted. It seemed like a test, maybe constructed for me to admit what I did.

Mark's voice also sounded skeptical, "But… what about the other PharmD students?"

"Vacation. Remember, they have September off." I did know that, since it was the Pallets' attempt to reduce burnout. It still led to more questions on exactly why the vacancy happened. Did the person die? Were they sick? Were they, all of a sudden, stressed? The cohort wasn't here, and the first year hadn't even started the program. Before I could spiral, Dr. Ilt spoke after scanning some colorful sheets of paper.

"We know that about 70% of confirmed cases are from Indigo."

Registering that this could be a test, and Mark was officially my competition, I spoke up, "How are they confirmed? Have we made a diagnostic test yet?"

Mark also chimed in, "And you said at Indigo. What other places have it?"

Milena hesitated, turning to Dr. Ilt before coming back to us, "There was somebody at Harlequin… and cases of colored eyes are pumping up globally—"

"And Taupe?" Mark and I both said in unison. We both knew about the cases we've been treating, but I was slowly starting to see more people who looked infected. They looked at each other before Dr. Ilt firmly spoke.

"Yes, we have Taupe cases. But Indigo has been presenting far more. They're running out of space at their clinics, and we know treating them as individuals wouldn't be useful like here at Taupe." I hardly knew anything about Indigo, but I couldn't imagine it being more stressful than here. Between students ripping pages from textbooks to a twenty-four-hour coffee supply, Taupe runs on anxiety and stress over grades and our future.

"How? How are they being treated?" My voice became low, trying not to convey panic.

"Fluids and general antivirals, mostly. But symptom-wise, they are all the same. Colors in the whites of the eyes, extreme fever, and body aching."

"Why don't you just send their blood here for evaluation?" Mark added, which angered me because it implied more work for us.

"Well… it's not as simple as that, right now. This is a virus that… mutates very quickly," Milena spoke as Dr. Ilt nodded, without saying a word.

It was odd watching the head of immunology not provide any sort of insight, the queen of viruses not say anything. When we were dismissed, Mark turned to me in Polish after grinning.

"So much for a nice and easy semester," he joked, which I laughed at politely. Instead of the lab being empty, I jumped when I saw six Pallet guards, in their red suit jackets, standing in a line and holding our backpacks. Milena appeared behind us, zipping her jacket.

"Oh, we mean immediately. We need your help now. As in, right now. The guards will take you to your rooms to gather your things," Milena said, behind us.

I prayed that nobody was looking through my computer or my print history, running any analysis I didn't know.

As we left the lab, I glanced at the PharmD door, thinking about what I was about to see, and whether it was really worth it. Since Taupe was in Hartford, we had to take a train to Northern Maine, where Indigo was. The Pallets had a private train for fast transport between the schools. Inside, red patent leather seats glistened as if freshly oiled. Sandwiches on Pallet glass plates stood in towers, alongside various bottles of water.

"Any beer?" Mark asked, which made him sound like an asshole. Milena replied in a monotone voice, unamused.

"No. Only water here."

I knew that the Pallets wanted to get it solved as quickly and quietly as possible. Milena was sitting across from us, with Mark and me placing our bags above us. I didn't know how long we were staying, but all I had were supplies for school and about three days of clothes. Those seemed like logistics that Milena didn't care about.

"This outbreak is worse than we thought," Milena interrupted the ten-minute silence on the train, speaking like a military officer. When she nodded to a guard, heavy folders were placed in front of us. We shared a glance before opening them. The first packet was a list of people, about thirty pages long, with what looked like ten people per page.

"We need you two to figure out how to handle it, how to contain it. It's becoming a serious threat to Indigo's population."

"Well…I mean, it's simple. Make a vaccine for it, and the lab can do that…" Mark looked up, before Milena shut him down quickly. We passed rain that seemed to follow us as we moved, falling as Milena spoke.

"Read it again, and look at the fifth and sixth columns." It reminded me of my mother, the coldness, the bluntness.

After scanning intensely, I recognized what the problem was in the fifth column. Each patient had a different virus entirely, albeit with the same symptoms. It wasn't just the one Moxy had, but a random assortment of letters for each person, all starting with 38FV. Normally, mutated viruses would have the same code, only the last two or three digits changed.

"So… I'm confused. You are having a… epidemic of…" I could feel my forehead wrinkles tense in confusion.

"A different virus for each patient, yes. And, it's gone global. In your folder are some cases, if you'd need them. All of them have wildly different symptoms, from fever to complete muscle paralysis. But, every patient has the whites of their eyes, the…" Milena seemed to forget a word, before finding it in a document we already read, "sclera. The whites of the eyes are sclera. Anyways, they have them as purple, blue, and sometimes green or yellow. Varying darknesses and shades. We're calling it the Bruise Eye Virus, or BEV."

Milena clicked open a bottle of water, which sparkled in the small lamp she had on her table. Bruise Eye Virus. I thought it was such a stupid name, since nothing about this seemed to be bruise-related at all.

"How is that possible, the different viruses? Because… fundamentally, that makes no sense." Mark and I toiled over the information that went against all our previous knowledge, that this outbreak was a different virus in each person. Every time that I handled an outbreak, it would be the flu. A flu virus, maybe some mutations, but one virus type. This document said that each person had a different virus, but the same symptom, which went against everything that we had learned and what seemed logical.

"Shouldn't you be telling me?" she joked, responding to Mark's question. For how successful Taupe was, it was frightening to see how dumb Milena was. How aloof and uninvolved she was as president.

"Well… wait a second. How do we know that these are the things… making them sick? If they all have different viruses, how do we…" Mark asserted.

"Because they have the same structure," I said.

"So, it's a mutation."

"No, it's a restructuring," I shot back

"Which is mutation," he replied, quickly.

"No, because mutation would mean that it would be the same virus. In this case, they are different."

"Right, that's my point. How do we know if these… genomes are the virus making all these people have… BEV… when they are all different? Sure, the symptoms are the same, but… it's an issue of casual inference." Mark looked at Milena and me, both of us were silent.

"Well… the only way I could imagine is… it would have to mutate from person to person…"

"Obviously." Mark scoffed, as if I were a child. Yet, none of this made sense, and mutated viruses would still have the same code somehow. The fact that the document said they were different raised suspicion. Milena nodded, somewhat impatient with the constant talking. "Right. So… that's why we have you. We need you to figure out how to solve it. And see if there are any health risks at Indigo."

"But… wait, don't you have Peter Cheshire-Yu? And…"

"Peter is running the data even more. He's the one who isolated it... well, them. He reported the virus and the table in front of you. But why outsource something that could be a learning opportunity?" Milena smiled at me directly. The fact that she was seeing this as an internship was alarming, and how much blind faith she really had in us. It wasn't until I reached the bottom that I recognized what was going on, and I tried to hide my startled confusion as I read one of the thirty-seven global cases that have been reported. In one case, Paulina Skova was a five-year-old girl with blue and green sclera. Except that Paulina lived in Michalovce, Slovakia.

The same city where my parents were bombed, the same city that no longer exists.

I realized that Paulina didn't exist; the Pallets manufactured her in a fake case file. I was falling down a frantic rabbit hole of mistrust as I scanned the tables and case files for other clues. I also hated how Moxy was right, that this virus was taking a life of its own by the Pallets. It might have come from my coding, but that was almost three weeks ago. It led me to question what was actually happening. How many of these patients were actually sick, and what was really waiting for us at Indigo?

Stepping off at the train station, it was a five-minute walk through the brick gates where massive smoke stacks towered behind. The air changed as soon as we stepped on campus, the putrid smell making my nose scrunch. Mark started to cough briefly before sipping a bottle of water and excusing himself. We were greeted by a horde of Pallet guardsmen in their red suits, standing in front of sad grass, brick buildings, and students moving through them in bland clothing. The guards took our bags and asked our names, before two other people in their late forties stepped forward in matching black outfits. Claudia and Caelum Pallet were the youngest two Pallet siblings, and just over a year apart. They towered over all of us, wearing heavy boots and having a military feel to them. Their garments were loose, with sewn pockets that Claudia reached into and revealed a watch. Milena went up to them and shook their hands, so professional that I would never expect them to be siblings. It was strange seeing the siblings have such a cold, professional relationship, one that I suppose the Pallet System needed to survive.

"Hello, everybody. I am Caelum, and this is Claudia. We are the Co-Presidents here at the Indigo School for Manufacturing. We were the first school in the system, and we have buildings here older than your parents." Caelum spoke so coldly that his joke didn't land. He spoke like he wanted to make you uneasy, and his tall stature didn't make me feel welcome at the school. They both, unlike Milena, had angular faces and under-eye bags, which gave an overall impression of misery. Claudia was less intense, being shorter, and I estimated that she was my height without her boots. They continued talking about Indigo's history, where Pallet glass is used, and how they make it. I would tune out, but I had to look better than Mark, who was eyeing the buildings noticeably. As we walked, I noticed the sour, sterile smell got stronger. I concluded it was a mix of rotten limes and window cleaner, further adding misery to the towering smoke towers we were walking toward.

The Indigo Main Hall, looking like a mansion from the outside, sat in front of four monstrous industrial buildings, which I assumed were similar to Taupe on the basis of a major per building. Again, I was corrected when Claudia explained that every student gets an engineering degree, with a focus on understanding Pallet glass in all its forms. Claudia confirmed how mechanical even the culture was by explaining the tunnel system Indigo had. The students walking in and out of the buildings didn't seem excited or even cheerful. They moved slowly and looked unmotivated, and while Taupe had passive aggressiveness, the students were aggressive. They rushed to class, and there were the occasional friend groups. Instead, Indigo felt isolated socially. Claudia held the door for us to reveal a multi-tunneled atrium.

"This is the Ventricle, or the Vent. It connects to each of the main buildings. The one in the far left goes to the dorms, which are underground, the far right is to the dining hall, and the four in the middle are to the manufacturing buildings. That is also where students have classrooms and have their hands-on learning experiences."

"And, we will be walking through there to go to the auditorium. We are right on time for the panel," Caelum added, not turning around to speak to us. His high-pitched voice was unsettling for how muscular and manly he was.

"Wait… the panel? What panel?" Mark asked, and I also shared his confusion. But I knew that it was time for obedience. I didn't trust the Pallets or Dr. Ilt, and Claudia spoke with a condescending tone that was refreshing to watch Mark feel the burn from.

"When did you think it was? Did you not get a schedule?" Claudia rebutted bluntly.

"No… what schedule…?" Mark seemed confused, and I was as well, although I didn't show it.

"It was the second-to-last page, behind the patient information. You have this today, and tomorrow we have a debrief in the Main Hall about the recommended next steps. Review the cases, and let us know," Caelum spoke directly to both of us, finally turning around, looking down, and in a low tone. Similar to his sisters, his irises were different colors: the left was dark blue, and the right was a bold, honey brown. Claudia as well, but she had a green eye and a brown eye. I was puzzled by this phenomenon, since the genetic trait for heterochromia was extremely rare. Claudia revealed the schedule that was folded in one of her pockets, a document outlining exactly what Caelum said, written in typewriter print with the red Pallet P at the top. We were given packets of case information and hypotheses, and I made the silent realization that this was all a fabrication. A fake pandemic, but solely a Pallet public health problem. This was all theater, and yet felt extremely real. As we walked through the tunnel to the alleged auditorium, I pondered exactly why the Pallets would want to get their students ill. They were their main products, and weakening us would weaken their credibility. I tried to be as inconspicuous as possible. At the same time, I didn't want them to suspect I was the cause. Was I even the cause? I kept going back and forth between the Pallets, knowing what I did and not when the dimly lit backstage was revealed.

Caelum and Claudia entered the brightly lit stage before us, silencing the crowd that stood in their presence.

"Hello, everybody. Thank you for being here today."

If this occurred at Harlequin, there would have been heckling or worse. But everybody stood silently. Obediently. It was chilling to see scores of students completely face forward, staring without noise, blinking, and occasionally coughing. Stretched over the walls were indigo colored banners with the signature "I" on them, with its sharp font type. They were banners that noted PBall cup wins, which I studied. I wondered how their players were, where they practiced, and how they studied at such a soulless school.

Mark and I were introduced as virus experts, looking at each other right before we stepped out on stage to a round of what felt like forced applause. Slightly delayed, and extremely uncomfortable. My palms were sweaty, and my leg bounced as we sat, luckily being hidden by the tablecloth.

Mark coolly put a piece of paper in front of him and spoke to the crowd.

"Hello everybody, my name is Mark Drykovczynski, a senior at Taupe studying immunology." He gestured to me, surprising me into standing.

"I'm Tadeáš, or Teddy Clawik. Also a senior in immunology. We are here to—"

"Help you all. To be a voice for you all, and to understand," Mark interrupted me, which made me sit back bitterly.

"What we can say is that… this virus is stress-induced. Our analysis shows that…"

Hearing Mark talk about it made my skin crawl, since it was obvious he had a better grasp of English than I did. The way he commanded the room without fear of being wrong or mistreated seeded envy, and his intellect made me hate him even more.

"The virus is activated through stress. And while we all are students… Pallet students at that, we understand that could be hard."

A soft yet noticeable murmur came over the crowd. Mark began to feel upstaged.

"Now, let's answer some of your questions. This is not about us… bragging or… saying how smart we are. We're all smart, that's why we're at these amazing schools…"

A louder laughter was heard through the crowd, before a line formed in the aisle. The microphone stand was joined by a line of about twenty students, the first being somebody in jeans, a flannel, and an orange hunting beanie I recognized from my dad's hunting wardrobe.

"My question is… with the Eye Bruise Virus, can we get… will we get some sort of vaccine?"

"Uh… well, our labs are…" Mark seemed uncertain and used a hand gesture to stall, prompting me to stand.

"Right now, our main priority is to create a test for it." I barged into the conversation and spoke clearly, "After we create a diagnostic test for it… then we can know who to treat and how."

"So my second question is then…"

"No. Next."

Caelum emerged from the shadows of backstage, to which the student cowered back to her seat. To watch a student cower in fear at him tightened the fear in the room. I felt sick being on the same side as Caelum in this case, and because I knew that she was going to ask if we had a test already, which we didn't. All cases were presumed from symptoms, albeit obvious ones, but having a physical, biomarker test would be the best way to know. But we had to understand why the virus mutated so much at Indigo. I wrote down an idea for a cortisol test quickly as the next person stepped up to the microphone.

"My name is… uh… Jonathan." A toned, taller student emerged who had a stained band shirt, dark gray jeans, and paint-stained boots, speaking with a strange-sounding accent.

"My question is… has anybody died from this?"

"No," Mark and I said in unison, turning to each other, with Mark domineering the answer further. "No, what we know about this virus is that it makes the patient… person fatigued and feverish, and related to stress."

"And while they have clinical potential to be lethal, we haven't had any such cases at this juncture," I added, realizing I sounded a little snobby.

"Thank you both. It means a lot, what you're doing." We all nodded to each other in respect, and Jonathan had a bouncy walk back to his seat. The next person was a frizzy-haired boy of similar frame, with an extreme amount of acne.

"Hey gentlemen… and Lady Pallet… my question is this…" He had a thick, southern accent, which set off alarm bells in my head. I have never met anybody with that extreme accent, and I only heard it in cowboy movies I would watch to learn English when I was younger.

"Where are y'all from?" he asked.

"That's not…" Caelum emerged, only for Mark to stay with his hand raised.

"No, no, it's fine." Mark had much more courage than I did to raise his hand at Caelum, who stood there with a tight jaw as Mark spoke, "I'm from New York, but my family is from Poland, Krakow, Poland. And, what about you, sir?"

"Kentucky. And what about that one?" He was pointing at me while I sipped the small bottle of water.

"Oh… um… Slovakia. Eastern Slovakia."

"Oh my God, we have two foreigners running this?" a voice in the back complained. This caused the speaker to laugh, and I could feel the color leave my face.

"Anyways, yes. I am Polish, Teddy is from Slovakia. But, the point that matters…"

The crowd erupted in horrendously mocking laughter, and I felt tears tremble in my eyes. I wanted to scream at them, to bomb them, to let them all cough. I wanted to personally spread more viruses, to watch them cough and plead. I couldn't bomb them, but I could make their immune systems explode. I could make this hellscape of a school a bloody, mucus-filled nightmare. That's what coursed through my head before Mark grabbed the microphone, before I grabbed mine, and spat furiously.

"Let me make something clear to you all. You don't have to like me, or him, or her. And, you can mock us and laugh at us. But we are here to help you. Because, let me ask, since you want to be so viperous…" Mark was shouting into the microphone at this point, to a crowd that acted like he wasn't there. It was like they were charged by him and his frustration.

"How many of you know what RNA is? How about a bacteriophage? What about bioavailability? Matter of fact, do you know why you should wash your hands, from a cellular level? You don't, and we do. You can grumble and moan, but the fact is… you don't know what is going to hurt you all, we do. And you need us." The lights turned on suddenly as the air became stifling, and an overhead speaker crackled, startling everybody in the room.

"If you do not settle down, we will increase the quota by 15%, enforced by red code." Claudia's voice boomed from the overhead speakers, which made the auditorium fall back in order. Only a creak was able to be heard, with Mark and me looking at each other before I spoke softly into the microphone.

"But, in all seriousness, this virus is stress-based. Just be… mindful and… aware of it. Thank you all." I felt awkward and out of touch to say, but the light murmurs of the crowd filed out of the building. Caelum and Claudia coldly gave their remarks. Mark and I found ourselves whispering in our native languages outside the auditorium.

"Jesus… what the FUCK is this school?" Mark wiped what I assumed to be palm sweat on his khaki pants. His breath was shaky, panicked, and different from my calm composure.

It was jarring, what the Pallets did, but after seeing the fake case file, I didn't put it past them. They probably did worse things to Indigo students, considering all of the products they manufacture here. I ushered Mark outside, a gust of wind pushing the factory scent into our nostrils as Mark kept complaining.

"And that… fucking smell. How would anybody want to be here?"

"I don't know… for Pallet acclaim? There has to be… something good. I mean, they leave with a great degree…" I thought about Jonathan or any other student being able to be the lead engineer on any glass project in the world. Whether it was windows to computers, drinkware to jewelry, Indigo students were sought after.

"Yeah, but at what cost? They get… abused all the… I could never come here." I thought about telling Mark about the file, but kept it to myself. He was still competing, but he continued to rant about the school.

"Taupe is… so much better. I mean, sure, we're stressed and worked to the bone, but… they wouldn't do that to us."

"Yeah."

I was suddenly questioning the pharmacy doctor degree entirely. Was I a cog in the lie machine? We hardly knew anything about the people in Dr. Ilt's cohort, and I imagined the workload would be even worse. We never heard anything from there, like a purposeful partition separated the good from the greats.

"But… hey, we're going to help them. These people are… sick and…" Mark spoke. I sat underneath a pine tree, which subtly blocked the smell. We spoke in English now, which felt logical and precise. "Sure, they are overworked, but… we have no idea."

"But, shouldn't we know about the students' lives? I mean, for contact tracing? All of our training and public health classes… told us that. Now, it feels like they don't want us to actually… apply it." I nodded in agreement.

Mark put his hand on my knee, causing my head to turn to him sharply in panic. I had never had a guy do that before, and it made me extremely uncomfortable.

I stood up quickly and spoke directly, with a slightly shaky voice in English, "I have to go. I will… see you tomorrow, at the debrief." I left Mark in silence, walking back into the Main Hall in front of the Ventricle.

I closed my eyes and tried to ground myself, deciding that I needed to go back to my room to embroider something. I didn't want to admit that Mark, with his spikey hair and cheeky smile, was cute, and that move he made made my stomach flip. Still, I remember the neon blue thread I bought earlier in August, and decided to add it to the inside of my sweater sleeve. Inside the Ventricle atrium, between the tunnels that connected to the dorms, stood a statue of a woman in the speckled Pallet glass. It reflected light from above, casting ribbons of blue and green on the moving students in the dark, mildew-smelling atrium. I approached the plaque that stood in a darker glass with silver letters, explaining who I was looking at.

Margaret Cheshire: Creator of Pallet Glass
During her senior year, Margaret filled her production quota and, with her extra time, began experimenting. Her fascination with glassblowing led her to mix multiple materials to create the indestructible Pallet glass we know today. Her dedication to Indigo can be seen in her story of hard work, dedication, and creativity that allowed her to change the world.

I was confused at the smiling woman standing before me, and I never knew that it was she who made it. I figured it was some Pallet ancestor, given its name, not a student. Indigo was not creative in the slightest, and I hadn't seen any student take time off. Each one seemed to be rushing somewhere and didn't exactly seem creative. Each person wore blue jeans and muted colors similar to Mark; it was as if Indigo mandated boring clothing. Yet Margaret was an advertised rarity. I thought about how overworked she must have been, or how efficient she was. I knew that having free time at Indigo was a fairy tale, and I wondered what they made before Pallet glass. I could tell that this was an example that Pallets used to market Indigo to deceive people into attending. I looked up at her face, her hands behind her back as she stared upward almost valiantly. From the smooth glass, I could tell she had a sharp jawline and a geometric face structure. Maybe it was the glass, but she also looked alarmingly thin, and so did all the other Indigo students. The students rushed past as Margaret Cheshire sparkled in the center, fully unacknowledged and ignored. One student went through a tunnel with the label VIAL LAB #4, which intrigued me. I knew that our vials were Pallet glass and could be thrown on the ground without cracking. I had always been curious where they came from, and followed the student through the tunnel.

Steaming machines and hundreds of vials moved on a conveyor belt as I peered in through the door. Students pushed past me and scattered throughout the scene; one grabbed a clipboard and jotted things down, another pushed some buttons on a large rectangular machine, and another tied their boots, glaring at me.

"Are you on?" a flat voice said behind me. When I turned around, a short girl in a blue bandanna blinked at me. She wiped her eyes as if she had just woken up and secured her safety goggles.

"Oh… um... no, I… I don't go here," I admitted shyly. I didn't know how serious Indigo was about other people in their factories, but she smiled at me to my relief.

"I can see that. Your accent is funny, are you from Russia or something?" She giggled.

"No, not Russia. Slovakia. Right next to it."

"Oh… well… thank God." She checked her watch before blinking at me.

"Wait a second, why does that matter?

"Cuz… the Russians are the Pallet Ball players."

I suddenly became curious, not realizing how Pallet Ball players fit into this school. "All of them?"

"Most of them, yeah. I'd say… over half. So, they don't work as hard or as fast. They're lazy as hell." I was baffled by the bluntness and tried not to be offended. "I had a Russian on my team once. Stubborn son of a bitch, mean guy too. But, you're from that… Slovenia place, right?"

"Slovakia, yes."

It was ironic that we both seemed to dislike Russians for different reasons. I had a deep-rooted, personal hatred toward the current government, whereas Indigo hated the people because they weren't productive enough and used for sport. The way that the Pallet System coddled these athletes across the system showed. It made me think of the social hierarchy at Indigo and how long this social class system existed. I wanted to ask more questions, but the students buzzing around me centered me in the factory environment.

"Are you… do you work here?" I gestured to the factory behind the door, with another student wiping sweat from their brow as they left. There was a droplet that came from their hand, which I assumed to be sweat. She blinked at me in confusion.

"Dude… we all work here. We work literally everywhere on campus."

"What do you mean? I'm sorry if it's too much…" I proceeded, feeling like I was prying. Not many Taupe students know the day-to-day of Indigo, or even Harlequin, for that matter. I'm sure she thought my nose was in a book all day or coding, and thought Cupid was somewhere on TV.

"Come in. We aren't supposed to let people in, but I'm forty minutes ahead of my schedule." She introduced herself as Daya and slammed the factory door open.

Inside, the air was hot and reeked of some sharp chemical, the one that permeated throughout the campus air. We walked past students doing various acts, mixing small beakers, typing, button pushing, and looking at blueprints. When I got to her station, with blueprints for vials alongside various documents, the girl pointed to a table full of numbers.

"This is my quota for the day. I have to… basically, run around all day and make this."

I scanned the page, finding out her name was Daya Rowing, and processed what I was looking at. Today, she had to make fifty batches of virus vials, thirty of bacteria vials, and fifty of blood vials. She had about ten items after that, all in another portion of Indigo. They were all various thicknesses and densities, some taller than others. It made me sick to my stomach to think about how many times I have messed up code, and Dr. Ilt shrugged and told me to toss it in the red bin. The number of errors our labs made, to think that somebody's grade depended on something we threw out. Daya could tell I was shocked, returning from doing some activity.

"Yup. This is my day, five days a week. Sometimes six, every other Saturday."

"How do you have time for class?"

"Oh, classes are from seven to nine on Saturday and Sunday, sometimes Fridays.

"In the morning?"

"Mine are, yeah. So I have the day to relax and not go to the evening one. My bunkmates all decided to do the morning one; we didn't wanna interrupt each other trying to rest."

"Daya!" a deep voice boomed, which caused her to go around the corner like a mother to a crying child.

I could hear subdued panicking and Daya trying to calm somebody down. I peered through the steel shelf of manuals to see another student, a slightly taller boy, breathing fast. I could also tell, from a distance, that the whites of his eyes were darkened. I approached them, and since he didn't recognize me, it made him worry even more. He pointed to my glasses, and Daya calmed him down.

"No… no, he's not with them. He's a Taupe student. He's not going to tell."

"Tell what?" Two other students stood by him, one putting their arm on his shoulder, the other listening intently. Daya spoke to the listener, who nodded like some authority figure.

"He… Lee accidentally added too much balancer into the mix. It means that… well, it puts him nineteen hours behind if he wanted the correct glass density." When she explained that, Lee got even more flustered, his eyes darkening.

I gathered from their talk that not all Pallet glass is the same, and thinner versions are used for vials, while others are used for sturdier options, such as my glasses. In this case,

Lee was tasked with creating blood vials, which were fairly thick. Daya called Lee to her station, which I assumed made her some sort of manager for the glass production. Was she Lee's boss?

"Listen, it happens. Do not worry, just log it and... we'll go from there."

Lee stood right next to me, calming down slightly after Daya gave him a glass bottle of water while writing in a thick marker. He accidentally bumped into my shoulder, and like clouds parting, his eyes became less purple as he blinked. Daya saw it happen almost immediately, and even though she discussed production logistics, he seemed to be calmer, his breathing slowing. She explained to him extremely complicated instructions, which he wrote down on his palm, but hearing all the things he had to do made me stressed. I backed away to read what Daya was referring to, only to watch his eyes go back to purple.

Daya stopped speaking and looked at me.

"What... did you unbruise him by touching him?" she asked, pointedly.

"Unbruise him? No... I don't know what that is..."

"Wait, wait. Lee, stand right here. I'm sorry in advance." Lee blinked with purple and green eyes as he drummed his hands on the concrete table.

"So, you added too much balancer, which means that you can only save about 50 percent of the whole batch, and that puts you behind on quota by..." Daya bulleted numbers, processes, and all the things he had to do because of his error. Lee's eyes darkened to a royal purple before Daya whipped her head at me.

"Grab his arm," she commanded.

Confused and frightened by her intensity, I placed my hand on the crevice of his sweaty elbow. His blinking normalized as, to our shock, his eyes went back to white after twenty seconds. Daya and I stared at each other with our mouths open, like we just witnessed a miracle.

"You…" Daya said, and before she could continue, I ran out of the factory.

Holding my glasses, I weaved between students with safety glasses. I abruptly slammed the door open, nearly concussing a student if they were a few inches closer to the door. I ran outside, the sudden rain overwhelming my senses and blending with the tears. I was so overwhelmed now, so scared of myself and the reality of what I just saw. Everything came together, why Connie and Mark relaxed when I touched them. I started this outbreak, and I was also the cure.

Chapter Four

I rushed out of the factory, being mindful not to touch anybody. I didn't want anybody else to know, but I imagined Lee and Daya were talking about it to their teammates. As I slammed the door, I watched a man, large and burly, walk slowly out of another tunnel. When I glanced at him, it was now a habit of mine to look at the whites of people's eyes. His looked like stained glass, streaks of purple, blue, and green could be seen from sleepy blinking. I stood frozen and still, processing this new type of case. He wasn't my age; he was easily fifty or older based on the color of his hair. Indigo wasn't only stressful to students but to professors alike.

I showered as soon as I got into the assigned dorm room, after navigating the various staircases and levels. I imagined what the other dorms were like, reeking of oil and sweat, dirty boots on the carpet. How miserable the students were, how nasty they were toward Mark and me. However, everybody at Indigo seemed to work well in the factory, so perhaps it was a work story passed down from senior to freshman. Or was it that every year, there were new players, and regardless of where their Slavic accent was from, they were seen as Russian? As I scrubbed my body, I thought about me being the cure. How was it that my virus, designed for reducing my stress, was now reducing others'? Moreso, I thought about ways to present the new information I had, thinking of multiple ways to frame it to everybody tomorrow. I now knew that my touch made people less stressed, potentially decreasing their cortisol, so some sort of cortisol test would be the best option for a virus that mutates rapidly. While I wanted to explore why exactly it mutated quickly, my fear would be to identify the very first mutation, ultimately leading to questions about origins. A soft knock was heard alongside the silverware clattering. I put down my pen. I opened the door to see my meal, which I frowned at. I guess the dining hall wasn't an option, because they probably wanted us to stay inside.

In a towel, I moved the covered tray inside almost on autopilot, as I kept thinking. I jotted down all of the theories of my own virus. I did have an advantage, having the code of the pathogen and being the first patient. If I were the cure for it, I would make another version of the virus, unmutated. I wrote down that my strategy was that we should monitor cortisol since Indigo students work hard. It made sense, since Indigo stressed out their students with their demanding quotas on all the various products. For everybody else, it meant that any sort of cortisol could make them sick. For me, I hadn't noticed any difference. I was stressed with school and everything, but I didn't have any sort of symptoms. When I couldn't figure out why I wasn't stress-free, I decided to have dinner.

The tray was steaming grilled chicken, jasmine rice, overcooked broccoli that turned mushy, a cheesecake in the shape of a cube, and a vase of flowers. I imagined what sort of mush the Indigo students ate, how what was in front of me could be seen as luxurious. I hunched over the desk and ate silently. In the rice, I kept seeing puffy under-eye bags, like Lee's. I put my fork into the cheesecake and thought about the PharmD students. Sure, they had September off, but what would they have done in this scenario? Would those students have handled it better? For all I knew, they were us but elevated in their coding knowledge. But nothing could have prepared us for the ignorance that was Indigo. Could the PharmD students somehow code away cultural bias? To engineer a bacteria that made people tolerant, or less tired? I couldn't blame the Indigo students, frankly. They worked all the time, constantly producing materials that held up the

Pallet System. I thought about Lee and Daya, and how they couldn't pick up a book when their entire education is solely based on machinery. I didn't remember seeing a library in the campus directory given to us by the siblings, which troubled me even more.

Restless in my room, I felt different branches of thought colliding. If the virus was stress-induced, I needed to see what truly stressed me, if I had the same one. I sat in my bathroom staring at myself in the overhead lighting, thinking of things that stressed me: homework, messiness, dirtiness, unwashed hands, and raw chicken. Impulsively, I threw all my papers on the floor, coating the entire room in a heap of mess. I wanted to see how I would react to the chaos, how my eyes would change into purple or blue. After about an hour of making my room a disaster, I gave up. I would check the mirror every few minutes as I spiraled. No change in my sclera. As I put all the pages back into a neat pile, I thought about other things that I could do to induce stress. One thing I thought of made me inhale and grab my phone.

"Cupid?" I said to him, answering before the last ring.

"Hello, T-Bear! What is up? How are you? I never get calls from you…" He was eating what I assumed were noodles, given the slurping noise coming from his end.

"Yeah, hey, listen… um…" As I spoke to him, my eyes weren't changing, so I needed to do more.

"I need to throw a party, a huge party, and I want you to invite everybody you know."

"Mmm!" His mouth was full, and he quickly swallowed before speaking fast, "Oh! This sounds like my sort of thing! What's the occasion?"

"Um… I… uh… celebrating life. Yeah, that." I tried to sound as convincing as possible, but any excuse to party was enough for Cupid. I knew that of all people, Cupid could induce my social anxiety.

"Oh, great! Okay, I will start to… wait, what if we did like a… funeral theme? Like, everybody dresses dead, so you… oh! Or…" Cupid rambled for a minute as I watched my eyes intently. There was no change, no matter how much he talked. Once more, I amped it up.

"So um… I want this to be… like… a rager. A huge party. How many people could… you think you could have?"

"Hm… well, your dorm is decent-sized, right? I think we could get like… fifty. Actually… let's invite seventy, because twenty might not show." I felt my eyes widen in horror, the idea of seventy bodies crammed in my living room, the smell, the germs, the sweat. Even as my heart raced at the image of it, my eyes remained unchanged. I thanked Cupid, saying I would let him know the dates and everything after I finalized my list. I hung up, closing my eyes and trying to truly picture it. As my heart raced, I felt anxious and frozen, yet my breathing fastened. In the bathroom mirror, I blinked the white sclera with my green eyes in the center.

I was brushing my teeth when my door knocked, startling me into quickly jumping into jeans and a shirt.

"It's uh…. it's me. Listen, I know this is… weird given how today was, but… I think we deserve a drink. I heard there was a bar here, in that… tunnel hall, whatever," Mark spoke in English, which was even more unsettling.

I remember how he grabbed my leg on the bench, and I wanted to ask him what he meant by it. Yet, I couldn't be distracted by him. I opened the door, giving him a look of apathy, "Mark, you have to prepare for tomorrow."

"I already did, and you… deserve a break." His cheeky smile made a part of me melt inside, and I puffed a sigh.

"Fine… but as friends," I reminded him sternly.

"No, no… comrades." He smiled, standing outside my door as I sprayed on cologne, put some gel in my hair, and left my room.

As I walked with Mark, who loved the sound of his own voice, I mused on what he would be like with Cupid. How their conversations would be story after story, each attempting to talk about themselves and maintain any thread of conversation. We found ourselves walking on the main campus, no longer smelling as strongly as before. Still, the hazy fog that cast over Indigo made it hard to see far as we paced. We stopped in front of the Vent, which had various advertisements and posters for Indigo. One girl in safety glasses, reading a blueprint and smiling. Mark scoffed as I watched two students walk past us with their heads down.

"There is absolutely no way that she is smiling at... her homework."

"Maybe it's really interesting," I added, trying to seem humorous.

"Yeah, right." Mark paused, suddenly becoming somber. "Nobody at Indigo is interested in their work like that."

Through a tunnel that was somewhat toward the center, it led to the Indigo Student Union, with its bookstore ahead and closed. There stood silver mannequins in the Indigo sweatshirts. It reminded me of the Pallet sweatshirts I bought when I signed my admissions contract, having to buy another suitcase to bring home all the Taupe merchandise I bought. Indigo's sweatshirt had white letters and small, red trim on the letters. Taupe was the light sand color with white letters, with green thread outlining the name. As for Harlequin, Cupid would wear the neon green sweatshirt with lilac letters and black and yellow threading. Right below the Indigo bookstore was a dimly lit set of stairs that led underground. Inside, it was what I expected. We sat at a metal booth with torn black cushioning, old posters decorated the walls, and a couple of students at the bar. I wondered if I would see Daya or Lee, but was slightly relieved that my ability to help people with the virus wasn't on the radar. There was a speaker playing some sort of rock song, crackling and definitely older than we were.

Mark left me and darted to the bar before returning to drop two beers on the table.

"This place is fucking miserable. I went to their dining hall, they only have single tables," he said in Polish, under his breath.

"You know we got food sent to us…"

"After my outburst, I didn't think so. But I was glad to see it waiting for me. The food here is awful, just… rice bowls and salads."

I sipped the bitter beer before swallowing, "That's bad?"

"Well, think about that every day. The mushy, bland flavor. Sure, it's fuel and healthy, but… where's the fat? Where is the bread and jam bar, like at Taupe?" he mused, sipping his beer.

"Yeah… I thought Taupe was bad."

I was trying to seem amicable, but deep down, I both hated him and liked him. He was an adorable obstacle, an annoyance that made me smile every now and then. Everything that he said irritated me, and my mind racked with every word to try to correct him. Which, candidly, was rare.

"But… how are you holding up with… everything? I heard about Slovakia…" he said, as I watched somebody enter the bar.

"I mean… I'm holding up."

"Do you have any family there?" he asked, blinking as if we were on a date. Was this a date? I was urged to say the truth about my family, but I pivoted to the half-truth for self-preservation.

"I have a cousin, Cupid. He's the only cousin I have, but he's at Harlequin."

"Great school, wild though, from what I hear. And he's from Slovakia?"

"Yeah, we grew up together in Michalovce. But his father is Ukrainian, and his mother is my father's sister. He speaks both."

"Oh… so a hybrid." Mark smiled.

"Something like that, yeah." Cupid did have a slightly different accent than me, slightly harsher, and sometimes would say Ukrainian words instead of Slovak ones. But I wanted to stop talking about my family for fear of being vulnerable.

"So, what about you? Do you have family in Poland?"

Mark sighed. "Yeah, my cousins… are trying to arrange travel here. Not to move, per se, but to… you know… prepare. They all thought Poland was next, but…" He drank his beer as I processed what he meant, with the word "prepare" being different from what I know in Slovak.

As we spoke, and had to rephrase sometimes in English, individual students came in and drank their beers in silence. Nobody flirted, nobody talked to one another. It was like a sad ritual. There was one person who, as Mark spoke about his grandfather, slammed the thick glasses on the wooden bar. He must have had close to four in a span of twenty minutes, and teetered past as he left. His eyes didn't look up, but his body just moved to the door. It was sad to watch somebody be so drunk and soulless, without friends or any sort of life.

"We have to fix this school, Mark," I interrupted, feeling somewhat emotional.

"Well… we kind of are…" Mark said bluntly.

" I get that… we have to be individually contributing to this, and we both want… to get into the program." The guilt was pulling me into any way to smooth this outbreak, to solve it as quickly as possible. Yet, Mark wanted it to be his trophy, the problem he solved by himself.

"Well… if there were two spots, sure. But…" He inhaled and put his arms behind his head to stretch. "I gotta get in," he said dismissively.

"That's fair…" I noted, quickly. I knew he didn't have the same emotional weight I did, but it dawned on me that maybe it took a case in Poland to really scare him. To actually see it as a problem, not a job.

"But hey, you're an amazing guy. Just… regardless, I'm gunning for it."

"As am I." I shrugged, reading his body language slightly. He was tenser now, now that I shone light on the obvious elephant in the room. As for tomorrow, I had no idea what was planned. I knew that Milena and Hawley, the CEO of all the Pallet universities, would be full of questions, and Claudia and Caelum couldn't care less about logistics. All they cared about was that we could help them and their student body.

"Another round?" I asked, trying to ease the tension.

"Uh… sure," he said, joyous at the idea of more booze. A part of me wanted to get him drunk, so he could be hungover tomorrow. But if he were like any of my relatives, he could hold his liquor. When I went to the bar, the short old woman poured beer from the tap. I glanced around, the dark colored bottles on the shelf, with the occasional bright yellow bottle, and the string of amber colored lights. The bar itself was sticky, and paper coasters stood in a stack near my right hand, holding cash.

The violin music sounded like polka music, which caused my head to dart to the old, crackly speaker down the bar. There, a man with gray hair and a large green shirt increased the volume by twisting a clicking knob. It was some sort of folk song, maybe something Polish. When I turned back to tell Mark, something was wrong. I felt extremely feverish, and my hand started to tremble. My breathing increased, and I would normally deem this a panic attack, but this was worse. The more I listened, the hotter I felt, the weaker my arms felt. I dropped the cash at the bar and fled to the bathroom. Pushing the door open, I was face-to-face with exactly what I expected. My face was clammy and slightly pink, with the whites of my eyes turning a grayish blue, with light green streaks toward the pupil. I inhaled, splashing my face with extremely cold water.

After some deep breaths and de-stressing, I went back outside to the bar. I didn't want Mark to be suspicious and think I was infected. I said I really had to pee, in a joking tone, and went to get the beers sitting at the end of the bar, where I dropped the cash. As I approached, the same song was playing. I politely and desperately asked the woman to change it as I felt my fever rising again. With her sweaty gray t-shirt turned around in annoyance, I realized what it was. The song didn't sound Polish, and it wasn't Slovak.

It was Russian.

My stress trigger was hearing the Russian language.

She switched the song to something Irish-sounding, almost like a sea shanty in English. I smiled and thanked her earnestly, feeling my temperature lower. I sipped my beer, and soon I felt a sudden piercing pain in my lip, pulling away dramatically as I stared at the glass. In my hand was a half-liter, Pallet glass mug. On the lip was a thin chip of broken glass, with my blood on the jagged rim. I had never seen a Pallet glass chip before. The woman behind the bar caught this exchange and immediately got another glass.

"Oh… God, okay." The old lady poured another glass of beer. "Do you need ice? Does it need stitches?"

I was oblivious to her medical incompetence. "No… it doesn't, just a small cut."

"But… I don't want it to be infected, you know. Everybody is sick nowadays." Her genuine concern irritated me, as I knew that any pathogen could be handled.

"I won't get sick, I'm certain. But thank you." I walked away with a new glass and my bottom lip glossed with blood. I sucked my lip before returning to Mark. He almost immediately saw the blood and turned white.

"Oh my God…" he breathed out.

"It's fine, just a jagged glass," I recounted, more annoyed than hurt. I didn't like the attention, and having Mark stare at my lip was weird.

"You didn't swallow it, right?"

"The glass? No, no. I'm fine."

"Jesus…" he said, drinking his beer. "This fucking school is hell."

About five minutes later, we kept talking about home and how Taupe students are stuck-up. He explained how his ex-girlfriend was crazy and accused him of cheating, which wasn't true. He asked me about my relationships, and when I said I valued school over boys, his eyes widened in shock. As he asked me if I had a boyfriend, I was facing the long entrance hallway, and saw a blue bandanna and a taller, familiar frame.

Shit.

I didn't want them to see me, to tell Mark what they had seen at the factory.

In a panic and acting purely out of hormones, there was only one option I could think of. I locked eyes with Mark and pulled his face into mine. I kissed him with my eyes wide open, his mouth and soft tongue tasting like beer, as Daya and Lee walked past us, around the corner. I was suddenly met with the horror of the situation.

"I… uh… I'm…"

Before I could even apologize, he pulled me again and kissed me with even more passion. It felt completely out of place, with my lip bleeding, the school draining, and the doctoral spot. Yet, I couldn't stop. I pulled away, seeing his cheeky smile, and told him we had to stop.

I didn't expect him to say how good a kisser I was, and how much he thinks about me.

I didn't expect him to ask to come over to my room, and hold my hand on the walk.

I didn't expect him to hoist me against the wall, moaning while he kissed my chest.

I didn't expect to get in bed with him, and for him to chew and kiss every part of my body.

I didn't expect after he left my room to get a Pallet Portal message from him, with just his room number and a heart.

Most of all, I didn't expect myself to actually want Mark to crave me. I didn't want him to stop; I didn't want him to compete with me. Lying in his bed next to him, all of my feelings toward him now realized. I had a crush on him, and finally accepted that. I fell asleep hearing his heartbeat, his thin chest hair pressing into my sweaty cheek.

Chapter Five

After seeing Mark's jeans on the floor, I confirmed that it was not a fever dream. I was, officially, in bed with the enemy. But my feelings toward him were extremely torn. I wish that this entire PharmD trial were over, so that one of us could get it, and he could finally ask me out. But I couldn't imagine us being able to get past that. If we were to be a couple, there would always be that tension. Between speaking two different languages and only one of us taking the spot, my logic told me it could never work. Mark was already awake, sitting at the edge of the bed, putting on his socks. My pillowcase, and the one next to it, were sprinkled with tiny droplets of my lip's blood. I didn't panic, because I knew it was due to last night. I pushed myself up, causing Mark to turn around.

"Morning... uh... how'd you sleep?" My mind was racing, and I was unsure of what to do.

"I slept fine. You?" he said, not looking at me. He stood, wearing the same boxers as last night.

"Fine, thanks," I muttered.

He went to the bathroom quickly, flicking on the lights and turning on the faucet. I hopped out of bed, noting that we had about an hour until the Pallets were coming to our doors. It gave me time to go down the hall, to pretend that it didn't happen. I jumped into my pants and heard Mark turn off the water.

"What happened last night?" I said, hoping he would hear me in the bathroom.

"I have... no fucking clue. I think we were drunk." I thought about my bloody lip, and maybe that soothed him even more.

"Yeah. I don't know why I kissed you, I just—"

"Don't worry about it. It was..." His head popped through the wall, toothbrush in his mouth. "It was a nice break."

I wanted to tell him that I thought he was extremely cute, funny, and snarky. Yet, with the wall between us, and him brushing his teeth, it felt wrong. I knew we were relatively sober last night and, if his upbringing was anything like mine, he has a well-established tolerance for liquor. I left silently, with Mark in the shower. No goodbye, no other words based on the night. We were now back to the same academic rivals, and now I had to focus.

In my room, I needed to shower to wash everything off me. To wash Mark from me, to decompress, to reset. Today was extremely important, and I didn't need this virus to work against me in the social dynamics. I flicked the lights on and pulled back in shock. The number of hickeys on my body was uncountable, my entire body looking like a mosaic of bruises. I looked airbrushed from the neck down, with shades of pink, indigo, blue, green, and yellow in various intensities. I would have concluded that it was the virus, some symptom I hadn't encountered.

But I knew it was Mark.

And he knew it, too.

With my mind sharpened, I paced my room until three knocks signaled the pack of red-suited security guards. This was my Pallet Ball tournament, my time to shine. Indigo's outbreak was the obstacle between me and the doctoral degree, the job with Peter Cheshire-Yu. We met Mark and his entourage, him nodding at me politely, and went up the elevator. I had no idea where we were going, but I knew that I had to be willing to defend my testing strategy. As we walked, I didn't look at Mark. Instead, I was finding ways to articulate how to explain how my lateral flow assay test worked, like a pregnancy test. Testing for cortisol was a good predictor. Since we deduced that stress leads to increased sickness, monitoring the stress chemicals regularly would be smart. That way, we could remove the stress and stop the virus from spreading. I thought about whether I had my test yesterday, after hearing that Russian song, I could have evidence of the stress. A number. A chemical. A reading for how stressed Russian makes me.

When we got into the conference room in Main Hall, three doors down the bar hallway, thick binders were accompanied by a bottle of water, a highlighter, a pen, and white sticky notes. Paintings on the wall showed what I imagined to be Pallets, given that each person had heterochromia and stood in the color red. Mark and I sat on opposite sides of the long table, glancing at each other every so often. He was still competitive, sure, but I was starting to feel consumed by his every mannerism. The way he listened to Hawley, the way he flipped through pages, the way he squinted at the projected slideshow as Milena spoke. Yet, I could not let this distract me, and I opened the binder.

It was the full and complete genetic code of the virus, from advanced mode. I assume it was the same one I designed. The first few lines looked familiar, which added to the overall dread of the situation. I felt like an artist looking at a painting he made blindfolded, and I had to pivot quickly in order to draw attention away.

"And, who is this from?" I started the conversation.

"Does that matter?" Hawley's eyebrows furrowed, and his sister twisted her head in confusion.

"I mean… yes. If the virus mutates, or if… it's host-specific." My relief overcame me when Dr. Ilt gave a modest nod, implying that I actually knew what I was talking about.

"It was… um… a freshman girl, freshman. We can get more information from her patient file." Hawley gestured with his hand, revealing a Pallet glass ring on his middle finger.

"Already on it," chimed Milena, who was texting.

Minutes later, a guard entered with folders containing her patient file, student information, transcript, and known contacts. The last document felt extremely violating, considering it had everything from bathroom visits to what she ate for breakfast. I read through her breakfast sandwich when Mark caught me off guard after Milena spoke.

"We now know the virus is stress-linked, and I wanted to ask what you two recommend. Now, keep in mind, we will be reviewing with Peter Cheshire-Yu and the PharmD cohort, but… immediate action is necessary. We have thought about a test for the virus itself, which has been tricky with its mutations."

"This is a wonderful idea, but you're testing the wrong thing." Mark's arrogance was on full display again.

Caelum and Claudia glared, seemingly unimpressed and insulted by the charades; Hawley and Milena, on the other hand, seemed pleased at the grandiose confidence.

"So… fine. What do you propose we do? And now… how do you explain that to Indigo students? They do ask a lot of questions…"

"After yesterday, I certainly know that. Well… I recommend making a test for this cortisol," Mark suggested confidently.

My eyebrows furrowed as I knew exactly what was happening and why Mark wanted to sleep with me. He looked at my notes, probably when I was in my bathroom in my room. Rage and betrayal fueled me, as the voice of my mother echoed in my head. She told me to never let boys distract me, and the one time I did, it cost me my entrance into the doctoral cohort. On fire, I began to harden into a cold scientist.

"But… what if somebody tests for cortisol and it's in the normal range? Or, what if they're an athlete with naturally higher cortisol?" I raised what I thought was an impossible question, trying to throw him off. As my mind raced, I felt like I was putting holes in my own argument, the one he stole.

"What makes this... accessible... because well..." he stammered, which made me smile on the inside. I could tell that he didn't study my notes so much as glance at them.

"Because I propose we could make a test for the pigments themselves," I asserted with my arms crossed.

"Yes, but how?" Milena asked, causing me to stammer longer than Mark. I felt embarrassed; diagnostic testing was always a weak spot in the curriculum. I hated learning about sensitivity and specificity and fell asleep in those textbooks. There were certain pages that had drool on them.

"What about this, a cortisol and four-pigment biomarker test, similar to... your standard... plastic strip... oh, what are they called?" Mark snapped his fingers, trying to remember, before turning to me and speaking Polish.

"How do you say..." in English, before switching into Polish, while motioning with his hands.

"Must feel good being runner-up in this room?" While I couldn't directly translate Polish, I knew the gist of what he was saying. My mouth felt dry yet clammy, my ears hot, and my jaw clenched. He was clearly trying to undermine me, but not seem snide to the people in the room deciding our fate.

"And how did it feel with me on top of you yesterday, or you kissing me? Or using me for my notes, you... pig. And the word is..." I said in calm Slovak before telling him about the word for lateral flow assay in English.

The room seemed intrigued at the collaboration, but a resentment inside me burned stronger. My face grew hot. I applied so much pressure when I took notes that I nearly ripped the page as I thought about how he didn't care at all. The PharmD for him was about status, not academics. I thought about that with my arms crossed while he presented on how we could test for cortisol and pigments that the virus produced. The only part I retained was that these chemical pigments made the whites of their eyes, sclera, change into purple, blue, green, or yellow. By the end of the meeting, it was clear that Mark impressed four of the five Pallet siblings and that I contributed one pigment idea that he further built upon.

Leaving the room, they decided on the basic engineering of the testing strip based on my stolen idea, as well as decided on the people who could design it. A general blueprint for the small glass test was made, alongside material chemists from Indigo, with the promise of pigment testing strips by the end of the week. I thought about Daya and Lee, how they would probably have more tasks, more numbers to hit. I left the room and wanted nothing more than to be alone, to pack, and to see Angel.

"Better luck next time, brother." Mark patted me on the shoulder as he walked down the steps. This was the final straw.

"Oh… shut up." I bobbed my head down the stairs. In the distance was a group of people; I presumed it was a tour.

"No, I won't shut up. I deserve this and I strongly… I deserve this." He cracked his knuckles loudly and shook his hands afterward.

"Deserve it? After stealing my idea?" I asked pointedly.

"Be proud of myself, yes. I did what I had to do. Do you know how hard it is? To… seemingly cure this outbreak by yourself? Your idea was good, though. And, well, your notebook was open." He stood facing me, a few steps below me.

"You are such… I fucking trusted you. And sleeping with me… for my notes?"

"I mean… I wouldn't expect you to prioritize a boy over a PharmD position. Once again, I did what I had to do." Crossing his arms, he spoke as if he made the rational, obvious choice.

"You know… fine, have the test. But you have no idea about this school," I spat. "Figure out how Indigo students

are going to take that test, how they're going to trust you…
or the Pallets. Especially after your little… episode
yesterday. Do I have to bring that up?" I had nothing to lose
at this point, and going after his jugular in an argument
nobody understood was the perfect release. He stiffened as
his eyes narrowed at me, realizing that I wasn't going to be
walked over.

"It's better than your suggestion… And also, you little
church mouse… at least I was assertive, and added to the
conversation." He scoffed, passing me on the steps.

I had to resist the urge to push him, to watch his brunette
hair tumble on the steps and crack. It was another frustration
that I had to infer a lot of what he was saying. It was like
talking to somebody and missing every fifth word, with my
anger left to fill the gaps of what I didn't understand in
Polish.

"Church mouse… you're just desperate for approval, and
need to steal. If anybody deserves this, it's…" The wind
blew my hair away from my forehead.

"Oh my God, we slept together once, and you're on my
ass. You're like… a fucking girl. Give me a break. I can't do
this with you…" He threw up his hands, and at this point, I
was almost shouting.

"Obsessed with you? Are you joking? Let's think back,
actually, you kept kissing me. My bloody lip, might I add,
you… fucking animal. Do I have to remind you of the
hickeys on my whole body…" I was about to lift my shirt
out of pure adrenaline when I heard somebody clear their
throat behind us.

Dr. Ilt revealed herself atop the steps, motionless with her
handbag swaying in the wind. She stood there, binder in her
hand, wedding ring sparkling in the sunlight. Her black
sunglasses made her look like a spider, angular and sharp.

"You boys are making this far too messy. Follow me,
now," she said sternly. Mark and I both looked at each other
and lowered our heads.

She commanded us in Czech, not English. And since it was similar to both Polish and Slovak, it meant she probably understood everything we were saying the entire time.

There had been a handful of times when I spoke Slovak with family in public and was caught. My father was extremely cautious about gossiping in public, whereas my mom was more lenient. There was a time when, at the Taupe bookstore, my mother was trying on sweatshirts and deciding between either the TAUPE MOM or just TAUPE UNIVERSITY sweatshirt. One was deep brown, the other was beige. That's when a woman came up and joked that the decision was easy, since they were both sweatshirts. As my mother pushed through the hangers, she hissed about how color blind the woman was and that she wasn't the one buying. That's when the woman snapped back in Polish, silencing my mother, who turned apologetic.

Now at Indigo, my seemingly secret language was much more serious. My legs felt wobbly as I ascended the steps, returning to the same building I had left minutes ago. We found an empty study room near the entrance, with a dirty whiteboard and the putrid smell of cleaner in an attempt to clean it. Dr. Ilt locked the door before her icy eyes beamed at us.

"Listen. I am not going to monitor… whatever you do, or sleep with. But you two… have to cut it out. Bickering in there? You didn't think they knew? Or… stealing notes? Oh, but because it was Slovak." She stared at me and then Mark, her head moving like a hawk. "Or Polish, you think that they didn't see it? You don't think that they told me about it right after you left?"

I felt ashamed and embarrassed that Dr. Ilt has understood me the entire time I've worked with her. The times I swore or muttered under my breath. Thank God I was so terrified of her that I never said anything. She scared me far too much for me to talk about her, but now, it was about to impact my entire career. My head bowed as she continued, with Mark staring right at her.

"I am not going to have my undergrads… my best candidates make me look bad in front of them. They fund us, and I don't want us to look… caddy. Now, here is what is going to happen. You two are not going to speak to each other, text each other, or be in the same room as one another past the ride back. I will be sending a work schedule that alternates between you two, so you can review the case files. Right now, you both have completely ruined my trust. That you both sound like the student at Ca…" Dr. Ilt stopped abruptly. She shook her head, her copper hair swinging smoothly before halting as she spoke.

"When I assembled my lab and threw students into the fire, I needed to weed them out. And even through your mistakes and miscoding and… attitude…" She gestured to Mark, who stood now at attention like a military official. "I kept you both. You were like me… silent, tough. But now… you are letting pettiness… take hold of you like the other students." She shifted tone, from monologue to interrogation.

"Why do you think I remove people from the lab? Any guesses?"

"Because you don't like mistakes?" Mark attempted.

"No… not at all. I mean, how many have you made? There were the countless vials you've lost, the coding errors, the forgotten badge. You don't exactly deserve a gold star in the perfect coding department." Dr. Ilt laying into Mark scratched a certain itch within me. I would have smiled, but when she stared at me, I felt like a mouse staring at a hungry snake.

"Any idea, Teddy?"

"It's um… because we're smart?"

"God, no. Well, yes, you all are smart. You wouldn't be at Taupe without smarts. But my lab, the reason everybody hates me? And hates you both? I don't tolerate petty drama.

The sabotage. My lab is competitive because I don't allow people who... adhere to Taupe's competitive mentality. The... undermining of other people. Sure, I do not expect everybody to hold hands, but... civility. I didn't want this...this thing to be a competition. I had my pick of you two, truly. But... the Pallets wanted it, saying that it was healthy to have some... competition. But, back when I was in school..." And she paused, like we struck a nerve of some kind. She bowed her head before snapping it back up and changing the subject.

"Forget it. My point is... leave Indigo. We're done, anyways. They're doing the test, now whose idea that was... doesn't matter. Go to Taupe, and no interactions with each other. Am I clear? Matter of fact, no. No lab work until the decision is made." Shock radiated into my chest, while Mark protested.

"But... what about the cases we have? How are we supposed to monitor the test results?" Mark whined, while I was too afraid to speak. It presented a valid point, since the other doctoral students weren't there until next week, and we would likely sort the data for reporting.

"I'll send them to Peter's lab. He can handle them," she rationalized.

Dr. Ilt pressed her hands into the back of the chair, expecting a nod from us both. After being dismissed, I wove between the wooden desks to the door, feeling Mark behind me. Dr. Ilt stood in the room, sighing.

The train ride back from Indigo was extremely awkward, and the three of us sat on different sides. They served us warm chicken soup, salad, and whole wheat sandwiches with some sort of delicious spiced sauce. I became acutely aware of the flavors, yet finished my meal first to grade the third assignment. I caught glances at Mark every now and then, who furrowed his brows at me, before he cleared his throat and read some documents. Dr. Ilt stared out the window with her napkin on her lap, sky fluffy with clouds. My eyes were glued to my grading, and I felt myself increasingly bitter and harsh in the marks I gave.

"Dr. Ilt, where did you go to school?" Mark cut through the silence, shocking me and causing Dr. Ilt to turn her head like an owl.

"You've probably never heard of it. It's a small school." She responded, sounding rehearsed.

"Which one? Is it in the US?" Mark pressed, which felt like he was defusing a bomb about to cut the wrong wire. I tried to pay attention to the paper, which was Hampton's, staying out of the conversation but eavesdropping.

"No… well… it was. It doesn't exist anymore. It got… it ran out of money, poor management." Dr. Ilt cracked the seal on a bottle of sparkling water, the bubbles hissing, before pouring it into a glass.

"Aw… I'm sorry… do you still keep in contact with anybody?" Mark pressed delicately, yet I was confused about exactly what he was getting at.

"A couple but… I wasn't that social at Cardinal anyways…" Dr. Ilt sighed, and the entire tone of the train car shifted. Mark and I shot a prolonged glance at each other, since Cardinal University of Medicine was an urban myth to so many Pallet students, and the rumor was that there were no living graduates.

"Since we are all here… seemingly becoming comfortable with one another, and I know your… bedroom activities, yes, I went to Cardinal. Yes, I know what happened. And no, I will not comment. What matters is that… well, what matters is I made the best of it." She bulleted in a list.

She began to over-fold her napkin three times, placing it on the table and blinking at us. There were mumblings of the first Pallet School that went under. Rumors swirl even still, decades later, on what happened. Some people say the Pallets killed students, others say they were bought out, and others claim true mismanagement. I could tell Dr. Ilt didn't want to talk about it, but there were extremely burning questions that I had. I didn't know she went there, and I would not have asked anyways. She wasn't an open conversationalist; she was somebody I was afraid of, somebody who mentored me. I returned quickly to my papers, glancing at the shifting Dr. Ilt in her deep red colored seat.

The car ride to Taupe from the train station lasted an excruciating ten minutes. Dr. Ilt's chin rested on her hand as she stared outside the window. Turning into the gates, a flock of people, some with neon hair, flooded the campus. My eyes widened when I realized what it was, and saw some holding microphones, others cellphones, some with note pads. Something happened at Taupe while we were gone.

Dr. Ilt rubbed her temples and turned to us in Czech, "Not a word. Just… do not confirm anything."

The few phrases of media training were nothing compared to the nosy, trained piranhas that awaited to acquire gossip. As I walked on campus, I made a quick right turn away from the huge crowd of students. Words such as "virus," "stress," "leak," "Peter," "comment," and others could be deciphered as I darted a swift right. The mass of students seemed to be on the steps of Main Hall, with some checking their phones on the pathway to the right. Luckily, that was the path to my dorm. However, unlucky for me, a pearly suit blocked me.

"Teddy? No… Tadeáš! Hello! I'm Tyle, a freshman at Harlequin. What a great honor…" A boy with cyan hair grotesquely mispronounced my name, with a heavy New Jersey accent. He walked at my side as I tried to keep my head down.

"No comment," I muttered.

"No comment on what? Just wanted a friendly chat, that's all." His tone was warm and fake, something I was not falling for. I was used to it with Cupid.

"I am not…"

"But… seriously, are there… do you…" He matched my quick pace, somebody fast and small.

"I said no comment. Please leave me alone. I am tired," I groaned.

"Tired from what?"

I got the sense about how tenacious he was, and I thought of only one method to get him off my tail. It was a risk, but if there were truly cases at other schools, the only way to have Tyle leave me alone was to make him sick. To make him stressed.

As if talking to Cupid, I snapped at him violently and watched his eyes widen in sudden horror. "I'm tired of hearing all of the rumors about you. My cousin tells me all about you. And he's heard some…. nasty, horrible things you've said. Some of them were drunk, others were sober. Do you have a comment on that?" I blinked at him, since my accent made the delivery even sharper.

His face became pale, and the whites of his eyes flickered pale blue. It was a risk, sure, but I figured that he must have had the stress virus. He stammered, probably from the sudden fever and acute body aches. More students noticed that I was stopping to talk to him, which made me almost jog into my dorm. That's when I heard him shout at me, which would have made me stop if I didn't have the chatter of more pseudo-journalists behind me.

"You sick bitch! It was probably you, you… you bitch!" His voice boomed, a trait that must have been taught at Harlequin.

I felt no remorse for him, and I knew his classmates were recording his downfall. In an effort to avoid people who were sprinkled throughout campus, I found a way into the Immunology Building, into the lab. I breathed a sigh of relief since nobody followed me, and they couldn't get in without access. I opened my phone to see a news article from Harlequin's Jester, their news outlet that was plastered all over the Portal. I barely read the Jester, since it never had anything to do with me. And yet, front and center, was Dr. Ilt's face and the nasty headline.

STRESS VIRUS TRACED TO DR. FREIDA ILT AT TAUPE, CHESHIRE-YU REPORTS

Dr. Ilt stared at me when she silently entered, going straight to her office. After waiting an hour, I walked home ready to melt into my mattress. Everything now felt in jeopardy: my job, my mentor's employment, even the lab itself could have funding removed from such a scandal. At my door, I stared at the paper frog with my government name on it, with a smiley face. I knew that Angel was my RA and made the door decorations. Next to my door, I stopped and tried to register what I was looking at. It was a photo collage of Cupid, taped on his door, with some of the photos falling off from the cheap tape. There was him with various hair colors I had never seen before, like green and purple. I was surprised that I hadn't run into him yet, since he had a dorm at Taupe that was right next to my room. When I could hear him through the walls, him talking on the phone or singing, I complained about it to Angel, who said that there was nothing she could do. As if summoned, he yanked open the door on the phone, my still presence startling him.

"Jesus Christ! Teddy, you look like a ghost, oh my God. Hammy, let me call you back." He was speaking English, hanging up the phone before sizing me up, noticing me studying his door.

"Oh, you like it? We do this sort of thing at Quinn; it's like… our business card. And, you see if anybody is hot."

Cupid stood in a black fur coat, with green jeans and an alligator skin crop top. He seemed foreign to me now, after our parents died. Cupid, every time we interacted, was bubbly and charismatic. But his physical appearance was similar to mine: dark, brunette hair, high cheekbones, oblong face. He did have considerably more height and muscle, which was another sore spot for myself. Now, he seemed to embody somebody that I had never seen before.

"I was about to grab some liquor for tomorrow, but wait. I want to see your room!" Cupid whined, my body suddenly fatigued by the overall lack of nutrition.

"Okay, only for a bit, I'm tired." I got the sense that Cupid hadn't seen the news about the virus yet, which I was glad about. I keyed into my dorm, able to smell Cupid's strawberry body spray radiating from behind me.

"Tired? No, you... actually, wait. Rest today, because tomorrow is Pallet Ball." Cupid grabbed my shoulders, our eyes locking. "And you are partying."

When I stepped inside, Cupid's face dropped at the emptiness. I had a barely furnished living space, with a single couch and a coffee table. He walked in and stood in the center of the gray carpeted floor.

"Teddy... what the fuck is this?"

I regretted inviting Cupid immediately, and found him extremely rude for commenting on the empty space that I had no time, nor desire to fill. "It's my dorm," I responded, plainly. It had a great view of the other fifteen towers, as well as both academic buildings, Khill, and Main Hall.

"You have so much room! Why don't you..." Cupid proceeded to bullet interior design ideas at me, which I nodded and affirmed shallowly.

He recommended white couches and glass tables, maybe a bar cart in the corner. His eyes lit up as he turned to me suddenly, almost manically.

"We have to throw a pregame in here, oh my God! Tomorrow! Yes!" The image of Cupid now colonizing my space, after taking over my school, suddenly made me snap.

"No! You can't just... barge in here and say what I'm going to do..." My voice was frustrated, my hands tense.

Cupid stood still, throwing up his hands in resignation. "Jesus, I was just..."

"Just get out! Go home! I don't want you here!" My tone made it seem like I was talking about my dorm, which was half the truth. I didn't want Cupid in my life at all. He wasn't supportive and barely understood anything about me aside from my accolades. From my standpoint, he was just the product of my father's annoying sister, her flamboyant offspring, an example of what not to be. Loud, snobby, pretentious, rude, and self-absorbed. There were countless times when Cupid's quick attitude was seen, and my parents would thank me for keeping myself together. But now, I watched as my own temper insulted him and his creative vision. With an expression on his face that I couldn't quite read, he walked out slowly.

"Fine. I'll head out… dick," Cupid muttered as he left, leaving me alone in the large common space of my dorm room.

My parents never really fought, except that one time when I was six. I'm sure they did, but my mother was so docile, and my father was so jolly, it rarely showed. But, after Avana made the comment at a dinner three days before Christmas, I didn't see my mother until the next morning. She silently made me breakfast, kissing the top of my head and recoiling, saying I needed a bath. I was too busy playing zombie games, a hobby I shared with Cupid that dissolved as we aged. She grabbed the car keys and came back later that day with two large bags in her arms. She silently walked behind my father, who looked at his beauty endearingly as she marched by in silence. For the next twelve hours, all we could hear was the sewing machine from the guest bedroom. My father took me to a movie that day, as well as took me to the hospital to wrap up some paperwork. I brought my video game, and asked if Cupid could come. My dad said no, sighing.

The next morning, I could hear tight bickering through the walls. The machine stopped, and I could hear my father enraged at my mother. She quipped back something about no privacy and no loyalty. I played my video game that day, and when my mother was showering and my father was making pagach, I went around the house. What happened in that room that was so damaging, so offensive? I was making my bed when I heard my mother go to the bathroom to shower, which gave me a perfect time to go into the room.

It was a coat. A sleek, jet black one with intricate, brown fabric pieces that looked baroque-inspired. Intricately sewn on, the tight silhouette, as well as the long sleeves, looked luxurious. Aside from that, brown fur lined the cuffs and inside. Even at the age of six, I could tell my mother was going to look rich. I knew my mother was talented with hand sewing, considering she was a surgeon, but this amazed me. I blinked at it, my eye level being on the hemline.

"Little nosy here, aren't you?" My mother's hair was wet, and water droplets were on her shirt. I could feel my face reddening. Her hyacinth and iris perfume radiated from her wet, freckled skin. She lifted me up, and we studied the dress together.

"Oh… did you make this?" I pointed down.

"I sure did. Your babka taught me how when I was a girl. I figure that… I want to still be good, right? Just like you and your soccer. You have to keep playing to be good, right?"

"Yep. That's what dad says," I confirmed.

"Yes, well… your father was right there. But I'll teach you how to sew, it's quite easy." She smiled and lifted me in her arms. I loved my mom's arms the most, because they were more muscular than you would think. I remember my dad calling us down and watching my mother with bitterness in his eyes as he slathered butter on the flat potato cakes. It was a poison I never forgot, but I knew it was temporary.

Two days later was Christmas, and we unwrapped presents. Dinner was the usual; we ate oblatky, halušky pagach, and other flavorless Ukrainian food from Cupid's dad. It was a culinary boot camp in both houses, and both mothers laughed at the figurative bomb that went off in their kitchens. With that, my father rose to his feet and gestured everybody to our living room. A roaring fireplace, Cupid and I sat side by side and adjusted our eyes to the room after the multiple camera flashes. I got the usual from Avana, more sweaters with animals on them. The adult gifts were always boring: clothes or a gift card for a restaurant I had never heard of. Avana opened her gift from my parents, her teeth stained from wine. I knew my father got her some sort of crystal vase, which she opened, but when she revealed the coat my mother made, his face dropped. Avana gasped in disbelief and asked if the coat was designer.

"Well… if you would call me a designer. Then, yes." My mother smiled, sipping her red wine and raising her eyebrows. She crossed her legs in her dark blue jeans, me to her right. We were on the couch next to my father, with my mother rubbing his back with her left arm.

"Angelika…you made this?" My aunt's mouth was wide open, her husband not truly understanding why she was so excited.

My mother nodded modestly. "Yes, I did. All for you."

"Oh my God, this is beautiful. What kind of fur is this, elk?" Avana ordered Cupid to put the wine glass on the coffee table, rubbing the elk fur lining gingerly.

"Yes, it's elk fur. It was a whole ordeal to get." My mother shrugged off, winking at me. It was something that we had, a sort of "I see you" gesture. And my mother did it quickly.

It was when I was fourteen that my mother told me about that detail, why my father was so upset. The largest elk he'd ever shot, from Poland, mounted in his study high above his desk. I never wondered why I never saw the elk again. Little did I know I would see it every time my aunt wore the coat.

Chapter Six

After collapsing into my dorm bed, I fell asleep at 7 p.m. and woke up the next morning at around 11 a.m. I could hear people crowding on the Dorm Green right below me, with the sun beaming on my squinted, freshly awakened face. At Taupe, there were four clusters of four dorm towers, set up like a twisted clock. The Dorm Green connected them all, and being in Hall Seven, I was the closest to it compared to Halls Eight and Nine. I stretched as I glared out the window, seeing a sea of dark brown clothing in random-sized clumps. The Pallet Ball game must have been today. Checking my phone and opening the Pallet Portal, I saw multiple students posting where they were, who they thought would win, and pieces of gossip. There was nothing about BEV, so I guess nobody was concerned about it.

It was still happening, even with the outbreak? I rubbed my eyes, groaned, and glared at my phone. Angel texted me and said she was coming over at twelve to pregame, saying how excited she was to drink after the long week. I had never been to a Pallet Ball game, and until last year, when Paul came into her life, Angel and I would sit in my room, mostly studying, and end up missing everything. I knew that Pallet Ball was a big deal, and players often got brand deals while they were at Taupe. After they graduated, pharmaceutical companies recruited them for public-facing jobs, like Faliha Prosper, who I've seen market health-boosting sports drinks.

For the hour-long shower, I frothed my lavender soap, which steamed the entire bathroom while some Slavic song played. I thought about whether I should even see Angel, but rationalized that she most likely already had the virus. The stream of water echoed so loudly that I couldn't tell what the language was until I heard the music stop. Somebody was calling me. I yanked the curtain to the side, expecting to see Angel. I heaved a sigh while I answered the phone.

"Hi Cupid," I said, shutting off the water. I looked in the steamed mirror and was startled to see that the whites of my eyes were faint blue-ish gray. I rolled my eyes and thought about whether Cupid himself, his unpredictability, was a mild stressor of mine.

"Rise and shine! Are you ready for the game!" he squealed.

I could hear other people in the background, probably some sort of pregame Cupid threw. I figured that he was somewhere, not in his dorm, considering I couldn't hear anything through the wall we shared.

"Oh yeah… thrilled." My sarcastic tone was quickly muted by Cupid's charisma. I studied the glass tile floor, yet another thing that was the same blue, brown, and green mixture.

"Listen… oh wait, they won't understand." Cupid lowered his voice like he was confiding in me, before resuming speaking to me in Slovak, "I just wanted to say sorry for yesterday. It was fucked up of me to come into your room and… tell you what to do. Lord knows… I would shoot you if you did that to me." I chuckled uneasily, knowing that he was half lying. He and his father were amazing gunmen, and I saw through Cupid's abrasiveness through his genuine tone.

"It's fine, I appreciate it."

"So… Can I come over to pregame? A lot of my friends are coming like… later, and Hammy couldn't get me a pregame invite, so I'm by myself," Cupid slyly pressed, while I rolled my blue colored eyes.

"You have a dorm." I was preoccupied trying to open my medicine cabinet with one hand, moving around various allergy medications, vials of old antibiotics I had engineered, to find eyedrops. I wanted to see if anything would help at all, even anti-allergy medications.

"Yeah… but it's so small, and I haven't set it up yet. I have no fridge or… anything. And you… you have all that space. Besides, how sad is it to drink by yourself?"

"I… uh…" I found the bottle and squeezed a stream of eyedrops into both eyes.

"So, it's a yes? Yay! Okay, I'll bring the booze, see you soon, T-Bear!" Before I could say anything, Cupid hung up.

What would I even do to throw a pregame? Considering it was me, Angel, and Cupid (and I prayed that it was only Cupid), I made my bed, tossed my clothes in my overflowing hamper, and stared blankly at my closet. The last time I went to a sports game was in high school, sitting awkwardly at a soccer game that I didn't care about, only because it was the last one of the season. Now, I was about to attend a three-team soccer game and decided I would ask Angel the rules when she got here.

"Teddy Bear!" Cupid's voice in the hallway shattered the peaceful silence in my room, followed by loud knocking. I was in the middle of making my bed, and was immediately irritated at him. Not only did I not want to see him, but I wished Angel were here to help me cope. I heaved a sigh before revealing Cupid and his Harlequin green ensemble. His arms and legs were covered in green glitter, and his cropped jersey.

"I had to ask Hammy for a jersey, so he gave me his freshman one."

"Hammy? Is he like… some sort of pig?"

"Hammy? No, it's Hampton! Number forty-seven." I didn't want to tell Cupid he was my student, and I didn't know their history. Knowing what I knew about Cupid and Harlequin, they probably slept together.

"Did he mind you… cutting it up?" I tried to steer away from the conversation.

"Oh no, he already did this, it came like this." Cupid's six-pack was also covered in glitter, and I laid a towel on my couch before he sat down.

Luckily, Angel knocked softly on my door moments later. She was holding a sign that said "GO PAUL, GO TAUPE" in brown letters, and was swimming in one of Paul's jerseys. When she entered, Cupid remarked that she misspelled Harlequin on her poster, saying she was rooting for the wrong team. It wasn't long before Cupid revealed a bottle from his emerald-studded handbag, and it passed around the three of us. As I watched Angel drink from it, I couldn't help but imagine that she now had the stress virus because of me. So did Cupid, but I felt more sorry for Angel, knowing she had far more stressors than Cupid. I just hoped it was transmitted when the person was stressed, and not by saliva. Still, the drink was an evil combination of some soda and vodka, which left us wincing after every sip. We left after taking three swigs each; the last one due to Cupid's immense peer pressure. I concluded that it was some strawberry soda that tasted nasty, and I watched Cupid take swigs of it on the walk.

"Okay, so… it's kinda simple. Just like regular soccer, you know soccer, right?" The air was crisp, and I was glad I brought a jacket, seeing goosebumps on Cupid's midriff as he interrupted Angel.

"We're European, of course we do. But we call…"

"Yeah, yeah, football, I know. So, it's like that. Except, there are two different modes."

"Modes?" I asked. It was all foreign to me, and I appreciated Angel's patience.

"Yeah, modes. Some people call it frames, like time frames, but… Paul told me only Indigo calls it that. But basically, there is light mode and dark mode. Light mode has the lights on and…"

"They play in the dark?" The alcohol was getting to my head, trying to piece together the rules.

"No, no. They turn on the black lights, so it's harder to see. Points are worth double, and it goes between those modes every two minutes."

"How long are matches?" I was in the middle of the group, almost ignoring Cupid, who was on his phone, sometimes bumping into people.

"Depends on fouls, things like that. But each half is thirty minutes."

Angel said hi to somebody she worked with at the library, the tall boy I saw when Moxy ambushed me. He didn't seem to remember me and drifted into the crowd of other people. I felt queasy as we passed hordes of students, all in various shades of indigo, neon green, and brown. At the top of the stairs into the stadium, I looked over my shoulder and marveled at the sight. It was a smear of those three colors, looking identical to my glasses, passing the library, the academic halls, and Main Hall. I smiled and entered the stadium, knowing that Cupid was parting ways and going to Harlequin's section.

"Thank God he's gone," I complained.

"Oh, be nice. He's your cousin." Angel's brown eyes were focused on me as we navigated to seats somewhat close to the arena.

I was slightly anxious about seeing Mark or Moxy, or any one of my students. I didn't know what kind of energy these games brought, but I imagined that it was a special occasion. The center of the arena looked like a pie chart, in each school's signature color.

"Angel… he's the worst. He's just so… draining. And… every time I look at him, all I can see is his smiling face when we were signing checks." I noticed that, during our trip to Slovakia, Cupid had almost completely changed. He became more abrasive, more apathetic. His jovial nature remained, but was coupled with a new greed for attention. When we got gifts from various people around the world, Cupid was grinning. I could only imagine where he was right now and who was surrounded by him. All I knew was that Harlequin's stand was rowdy, and from the people I saw from a distance and on the huge screen, it was his type of crowd. A girl with blue hair flashed the camera before quickly cutting to straight-faced Indigo fans with their beer.

"You doing all right with the…" Angel asked in a low voice.

"BEV? I mean, sure, but I have no idea why they're here."

"They?" Angel's head turned.

"Indigo. They're slammed with it, and cases keep going up. I don't get why they didn't cancel."

As I shrugged and Angel rubbed my arm affectionately, the lights above the seats dimmed, the blue and brown sections mellowed, while it seemingly charged the electric green students.

"Ladies and gentlemen, please welcome to the field, the Pallet family!" a voice boomed, and thunderous applause erupted while five distinct people walked onto the field. The four I saw yesterday walked out first, all in matching red. I sneered as I saw Caelum and Claudia, knowing the truth about their manufacturing school. In the center of the field, Milena grabbed the microphone and began speaking.

"Hello everybody, and welcome to this year's first Pallet Ball game!" Her lips were a putrid, clownlike red. It was clear that Claudia had the only sense of style, being the youngest, and watched her sister with a polite smile as she continued.

"We are excited to see all of you, and can't wait to get it started…" A low boo came from one of the sides, and it wasn't until I scanned the arena to see that it was coming from Indigo's side. I looked at Angel, who was puzzled, before watching Hawley speak into the microphone. I knew why they were booing.

"Thank you, Milly. As you all know, I am Hawley Pallet, President of the Corporation. It's times like this when…we see how integrated we all are. How… cohesive the schools are together. I am beyond excited to see how the match plays out." Hawley passed the microphone to Caelum, only to have Claudia almost obviously snatch it away from him.

"Indigo will win, thank you very much. Just like last year," Claudia said, as deadpanned as I could imagine.

I wondered if any of their players would have colored eyes or would be sick. There was something so brutal about her and Caelum, like they did not match the family at all. The other three were fairly upbeat, but the younger two wore scab red with black hair. Filmore, the oldest, was the president of Harlequin. When he grabbed the microphone, I had to cover my ears from the noise. The screen showed Harlequin fans blowing kisses to Filmore; one sign was just his face, and the footage returned to him speaking.

"Wow... what a welcome! See, the Jesters are no laughing matter; we are no joke! But, all kidding aside, I know the green will take it home. Guys, let's meet our teams, yeah?"

He passed the microphone to Caelum, who scanned the crowd slowly.

"We are pleased to announce the blue turf...The Indigo Swordfish." Like a flight of bats, deep indigo jerseys painted the blue sand portion of the field. My face was squinting at all their faces, yet I was so far away that I could barely see. Military-style clapping was heard, almost in sync, as I watched them. Their thirty starting players stood in a line, with their hands behind their backs. All were relatively muscular, contrasting with the factory workers I saw. Even Angel was shocked at how uniform they were.

"Jesus, do they electrocute them?" She sipped from her glass bottle of water.

"Or, are their bones made of glass?" I quipped back, knowing the truth.

We called them glass blowers, but apparently, that was derogatory and belittled the Pallet School to something fragile. Plus, everybody called Taupe nerds and Harlequin students druggies, but Indigo got particularly offended by their term. When Indigo finished filling out the field, Angel joined me in covering our ears when Filmore got the microphone, and I knew it would be a deafening circus.

"Thank you, guys. Very happy to see you swordfish… swim on the field. Now, I would like to welcome MY TEAM. THE TEAM. We are no joke, we are no laughing matter. Please welcome, all the way from New York City, The Harlequin University Jesters!"

At first, nobody came out. Harlequin's section was extremely silent, and the lack of noise made the arena seem eerie. Then, a low hum could be heard from the back of their side and grew louder. I uncovered my ears and listened to what was happening. They were chanting "HA" slowly, astoundingly menacing and taunting like laughter.

It wasn't long before it seemed every Harlequin fan was screaming HA, which caused the white lights to come back on and an explosion of green spilled on the lush grass, with every color of hair imaginable. The Harlequin players flipped, backflipped, ran, danced, and leapfrogged on the field. The lights alternated between white and purple, almost strobe-like, and made my eyes hurt. They were all smiling and laughing, blowing kisses at the crowd and pointing to their adoring and screaming fans. There were guys with green buzzed hair, girls with wild-colored braids, and guys with neon yellow nails. Some had their jerseys cropped, others wore knee pads the color of highlighters. Hampton was clapping and skipping before landing into a split and winking at the camera. Admittedly, it was very exciting to watch, and he was really cute.

The noise subsided until the microphone was given to Milena, who turned to our section.

"That was noisy…"

The green smear booed, and the players looked at the audience for their reactions. Even Filmore acted hurt theatrically, grabbing his chest and seemingly stealing

Milena's attempt at attention. It made Taupe look bad, since everybody was cringing at our president.

"Please welcome to the stadium… Taupe University's Kangaroos!"

Our side erupted in cheers and claps, louder than Indigo by a long shot. Cannons blasted, and Taupe players ran on the field, with a normal amount of enthusiasm. They looked like professional athletes, not trying to entertain but to win. Paul flashed on the screen briefly and waved to the camera. Angel jumped and screamed, waving her sign above her head. Angel said that we all said "roo" instead of cheering toward the end, given our mascot.

"So… once again, for those who have never been before, this is how the game works. We will place the Pallet Ball in the center, and at the sound of the horn, the game will start. We will have a halftime at thirty minutes, and then resume for the last thirty. Now…"

Milena revealed the Pallet Ball, a fluorescent red orb smaller than a soccer ball. Milena passed it to Hawley, who placed the ball in the center of the turf. Milena then addressed all the teams by turning while she spoke, her hands collapsed in front of her.

"As the president of Taupe, thank you for being here. And good luck!"

The Pallet siblings walked off to applause and cheers, with a louder boo coming from Indigo's side. There was no camera coverage, but I could tell the Harlequin students were taunting the other players from behind their line. I could only imagine the things they were saying, but after about twenty seconds, the lights flickered to a deep purple, UV light.

I pointed and asked what each stadium part was, because they all looked different.

"Oh… uh, Taupe's side is dirt, Harlequin's grass, Indigo's dense turf sand. So they wear special cleats and have different roles. Like, Paul has really sharp cleats because he's on Harlequin's offense."

"He has to face the clowns? Good luck." Angel laughed at my joke, and the game started.

When the horn sounded, a dispersion of the players occurred. An Indigo player reached the ball first, only to have a tall girl in yellow face paint slide to the ball and swing her leg around, tripping the player. She darted to the Indigo goal, slowed down by the sand, only to cartwheel a hard left to avoid a player, with the ball seemingly sticking to her leg.

"What the…" I said, while my eyes darted at the chaos and the laws of physics being broken.

"Magnetic shin guards. And on the sides of their shoes. It's to do tricks, mostly for offense." Angel shoveled popcorn in her mouth, washing it down with a canned drink, as her white neon teeth glowed under the light.

The first goal in the first half was for Taupe, with a giant player, who I think was in the class I TA, with a noticeable mouth guard, charging at Indigo's goal. He side swept with the ball, evaded a small Harlequin player that slid underneath, and another Indigo player that tried to cleat him in the thigh. When he launched the ball into Indigo's net in dark mode, I watched the white lights turn on and Taupe swarm to the blue-sanded side. The players in their brown jerseys looked like seaweed, and I could not stop Angel from screaming in my ear.

There was a minute left in the first half when some sort of foul happened against an Indigo player and a Harlequin player, stopping the game and switching to normal light mode. At this point, Taupe had five points, Harlequin had three, and Indigo had two, and the cameras zoomed in on the altercation between the players. The referee was a short man and futile in trying to dispel the dispute. It seemed heated, yet I couldn't read their lips.

"What are they saying?" Angel asked, also confused. Paul was standing across the field near Harlequin's goal, while the interaction was happening toward Indigo's goal.

"I have…"

"It's probably Russian." A person in front of us turned around, remarking matter-of-factly, "I heard all their players are from there. So..."

I remembered the conversation with Daya and tried to read the lips of both players. Then, the Harlequin player pulled down their eyes and pointed, saying something that irritated the Indigo player. I felt my chest rattle with anxiety, and my heart started to race. Both players got escorted off by Pallet guards, escalating to such a vile interaction that the Pallet logo replaced the footage on all screens. The game started shortly after, with a Taupe player running with the ball, now glowing under the UV light.

"That was... wild... whoa." Angel turned to me, her face expressing concern.

"Teddy, your eyes are..."

I shook my head, knowing exactly what was happening. I knew it was because they were speaking Russian. I felt ashamed because I knew that I had it, and now Angel did, too. I knew that my BEV was showing, but when Angel held up a mirror, I blinked profusely to understand what I was seeing.

From the UV light, my eyes were glowing a bright, fluorescent green. The rest of my face was purple as I continued to study my eyes. It was a milky, glowing green with streaks of what I assumed to be blue or purple. I pushed past the people in the row, keeping my head down out of embarrassment, and went to exit. Angel called from behind me, following me outside the roaring arena. My heart was beating so fast, and my legs wouldn't stop walking. I found myself standing outside the Khill Library, with Angel's sneakers making a rubbery noise behind me.

"Teddy! Teddy...wait!"

"No, Angel just..." I stepped away from her, knowing that I was infected; she was too. She had to have known that, since now it was a matter of contact tracing. She drank from my bottle; we were right next to each other. If she didn't have it before, she had it now.

"Teddy… everybody has BEV, it's…"

"No, they don't! They can't all have it!" I pulled my hair up, feeling my warm forehead as I realized how much of a disaster it was. The virus was spreading, and now it was becoming normalized. Worse than normalized, it was becoming used as a tool. For what, exactly, I didn't know. But, I didn't want Angel to be a part of it, to be roped into a guilt and anxiety-filled game. I found myself slouched on a bench, Angel rubbing my back.

"You should go back in there. Paul's probably…"

"Paul could be winning the whole damn game, I don't care. You precede him."

"Those fucking… Russians. That's what did it to me. That's my fucking… stressor."

"Oh, that's not your… stressor." Angel sat up, almost as if to correct me.

I scoffed, lightly. "Yes, it is, believe me. It…"

"No, a stressor is Cupid, or grading. Those don't give you the eye colors, do they?" I shook my head, simultaneously intrigued by where she was going.

"But, at least my lab thinks, this virus isn't just stress-based. It's trauma." The breeze gusted and swayed the pine trees, filling my nose with the woodsy aroma that reminded me of home.

"Wait, what?" I sat up, intently listening to Angel.

"Oh yeah, everybody says it's stress and cortisol and… blah blah blah. But it's not that. Well, sure, we think it might be cortisol, but… It's trauma-based, not stress-based."

"How… how do you know that?"

"Our labs are doing the research behind it. The Pallets are pressing us like crazy to figure it out, well, figure out the patients."

"Oh… I didn't know that. Did you guys find anything?"

"No, but..." Angel wrapped her arm around me, as I looked at her pensively. "I'll let you know when we do."

I asked Angel to sit for a minute so I could calm down, which in reality meant that I wanted to think. I never thought about it being trauma-based, and maybe that was the entire flaw. I was so fixated on stress that I completely disregarded trauma, didn't even think that it could have anything to do with the immune system. Besides, as I watched the clouds pass, I thought about how I didn't even think about Russia as traumatic, only stressful to hear. Was my stress virus not even stress, but somehow reacted to trauma? If that was the case, were all the patients somehow traumatized by the Pallets?

We went back inside, and I promised Angel to let me know if my eyes changed again. When Taupe won, I got a moderate boost of excitement and cheered with Angel. She was ecstatic, and everybody on our side seemed elevated overall. After Taupe won and the green-wearing players were no longer as cheery, we waited outside the arena by text instruction from Cupid. I could only imagine the inebriation that he would be, considering there were slews of students from every school that was teetering or being held up by their friends. The worst part was that it was only 5:30, I was in no mood to party, and that the parties would be starting around ten. I wanted to go to the lab, to comb through the code and see what made trauma chemically and immunologically different. Paul and Angel were standing there too, drawing crowds with congratulatory messages from people to Paul. Angel was in the middle of speaking to a girl in pigtails when Cupid's voice boomed behind us. "Let's hear it for the...." He cupped his hand and chuckled after. "ROOS," people around him echoed.

He cackled, sounding like a mix between a hyena and a witch. Moments later, a defeated Hampton emerged with the soil on his face, and his cleats draping around his neck. He descended the stone steps, which were yards long and were a camouflage of various blues, browns, and greens, and it wasn't long before Cupid cracked a can for him on the walk to my room. Hampton and Cupid talked about which guys they thought were hot. Angel and Paul were walking in front of me as well, which left me behind them, contemplating the virus. It was agreed that we would pregame the parties at my place around eight, but until then, everybody split up into pairs.

"Hey, so…Hampton and I were wondering if we could have the pregame at your place? I mean, you live alone, right?"

"Yeah, I do… I just don't like having a lot of people in my dorm. It's a me thing."

"But you guys just won! And, you should celebrate! And you wanted to throw that funeral party. Plus, it's one of your last games here at Taupe, so you have to end on a high note."

Cupid's eyes blinked rapidly at me, and it became clear after every point I made, every reason I was uncomfortable, Cupid had a counter reason. I heaved a sigh and reluctantly agreed to host a few people. I told Angel that I wanted to be alone, to emotionally prepare for the evening. She told me, by whispering in my ear, not to worry about the virus. That everything would be okay, and that worrying about it would make it worse.

I should have clarified what a few people meant, because to Cupid, it must have meant thirty people who flooded my dorm all at once around 10 p.m. I told Cupid he could come at 8:30, but he apologized with a case of WinkDrinks, some drink from Harlequin that he managed to smuggle, which Angel and I opened in my room.

The night pregame drew more people that I didn't know. Angel showed up with Paul and about five other PBall players, who graciously thanked me for hosting, and Hampton invited members of his own, who branded me as Tadpole. I was introduced to Janis, who played on Harlequin, wearing neon green braids that hung down her black two-piece snake skin set, with necklaces made of some sort of yarn. I met Max, who was studying neurology at Taupe, who ended up talking to Angel about how much they didn't like a new professor. Cupid and Hampton drew their own crowd on my couch, with two girls and two guys, who were enamored by Cupid speaking Slovak. He was flirting, of course, and flagged me over at one point. Shuffling through the people, I stood directly in front of him. His iridescent green eyeshadow matched his glittering green eyes, and he blinked as he asked me to explain why Slovak people were superior lovers.

"Oh… uh… I mean… we're nice…?" I said, awkwardly and not fully understanding what to say.

"You are? Then Cupid's not from there!" Hampton said, getting a laugh from those around him. The speaker, which somebody brought, played music that sounded like a fire alarm.

"I mean… the language is sexy, right? Guys must've loved it when you spoke it." Cupid batted his eyes at me, waiting for me to pay him a little attention.

"Oh… absolutely…" I smiled and poured shots for the five people in the conversation.

"How do you say cheers?" one player asked.

"Oh, it's—" Cupid started, but I interrupted and spoke Slovak to the group.

I raised a glass and looked directly down at Cupid and said, "Most Slovaks are nice," and threw the shot back, walking away. I could hear the round of Harlequin students parroting my Slovak phrase, and teaching their friends a phrase I knew plunged a knife into his ego.

I snuck into my bedroom at one point with Angel, to catch up and tell her everything about Cupid. The music could be heard down the hall and through the thin walls,

"How are you two… related?" I was surprised Angel was even there, but because Paul was on the team and they won, she sacrificed her introverted self to be supportive. She sipped her can, which had a Harlequin player printed on it.

"I have no idea... It's like he's from another planet."

"Has he always been—"

"Intrusive? Rude? Disrespectful? Absolutely. I mean, he would constantly try to cheat off me in school, and talk back to teachers."

"And like... right, how is he related, anyways? Because like, I have cousins that are just like... friends. You two... sort of look alike? But, not really."

"Yeah, he's my actual, blood cousin. My father and his mother are siblings."

"Right... you okay, though? I know today was a lot."

"Me? Yeah, this is... fun. It's different, I guess, but I needed this distraction. Thank you." I hugged Angel, who sat on my gray comforter.

I resumed sitting on my desk chair, glad to have a break from all the people, assessing how Angel looked the part of Pallet Ball girlfriend. She wore a top that looked like a t-shirt over her boobs, and flared out orange pants. My closet was a boring coagulation of gray, blue, green, and black.

My room was also boring, with immunology books, no paintings, no posters. Angel's room had photos of her, her bunny, us, her parents, her grandma, and postcards from every place she traveled to. She had lights that looked like tiny gemstones that glowed various colors, making her room full of color, full of personality. She had one from when she visited me in Slovakia last year, with the Tatras glowing in front of a rising sun. Still, I saw my room as simple and a vacation from the noise.

The Pallet Ball Dorm Halls, which were halls ten and eleven, were especially loud tonight, since it was a fourteen-story building that housed all 400 players. There were flashing colored lights out of every window, and people funneling into the entrance lobby. Even though it was identical to the other dorm towers, it felt cooler, less academic. Luckily, Paul brought Angel and me through the back, mandating to Cupid that he could only bring two other people. He was fine with this and brought Hampton and a green-haired boy-looking person I didn't know. Paul lived with other offensive players, and their suite was crowded with both students and players. Of course, Cupid saw somebody he knew and left us. I stayed by Angel's side, who was close to Paul the entire night. I scanned the room and saw Indigo students chugging beer at an impressive rate. I saw girls with bright colored hair take pills sneakily, chasing them with a clear bottle they passed between them. Taupe students awkwardly danced to the beat of some electronic music, and the DJ was some girl who wore white nails and intense eye makeup.

"Are you having fun still?" Angel asked, blinking at me.

"I mean… I am painfully sober," I replied, shouting over the music.

Angel nodded, grabbed my hand, and brought me to the kitchen. Cupid was sitting on the counter and playing with someone's dreads. I cracked open another WinkDrink, which was housed in my denim jacket, starting to feel the energetic buzz. WinkDrinks were alcoholic energy drinks, so I felt both tipsy and caffeinated, jittery yet confident. With Angel flirting with Paul, and Cupid flirting with his boy, I whipped my head around. How would I even pick somebody up? I thought about Mark and Indigo, but he would never come to this kind of party. I had never flirted with anybody openly before, nor had I gone to a party, either, but it felt like the first time where I could. Maybe it was the WinkDrinks or the virus pressure being gone, but I finally felt free. My eyes darted around the room, and I unbuttoned two buttons on my shirt to really feel scandalous. After I did that and sipped my drink, I noticed Angel grab my hand.

"I need to pee."

"Now? But… I want to dance!" I dragged her to the makeshift dance floor, only to be pulled slowly near the bathroom line.

"No… I need to pee… now."

I groaned as I followed her through the narrow hallway, through the cluster of diverse students. There were Harlequin students in mini skirts kissing Indigo students in flannels, Taupe students were talking with each other amicably, and there were two girls in different Pallet jerseys making out. Normally, this would be an infectious disease nightmare, something I would read about as a super spreader. But I just laughed, realizing that everything was fine and stress-free. This virus, whether stress or trauma, was all in my head. I had control over it, and there was nothing to worry about. That, the entire time, stress came from within, and that everybody in the Pallet Schools wasn't out to get me.

Chapter Seven

Dr. Pellin's class was a harsh stress reminder that I didn't miss, on a Monday, nevertheless. Now that I had a break from the outbreak, I had to attend Dr. Pellin's class and give it my full attention. The cold calling, the expectation to give perfect answers. He flatly called a girl unprepared because she mixed up two scientists. She sat back down, biting her nails and fidgeting. The lecture was on the history of the field and how Taupe pioneered with the brain mapping technology. When Dr. Pellin, in an ugly yellow suit, asked Angel a question, she blinked anxiously.

"I… uh…"

Angel hadn't been fully paying attention, but instead was doing RA paperwork. There were a number of incidents that occurred after the campuswide party, Angel reported to me before class started. As for Cupid, I didn't ask him to overshare explicit sexual details at 11 a.m. Yet, he hooked up with some Taupe students in Hall Twelve, and it was wonderful. My head turned to Angel, whose panicked eyes darted across the lecture screen with her pen hovering over a report form. Between her job at Khill, the RA job, the lab work, and class, Angel was almost always multitasking.

"Did you hear my question, Miss Marsa?"

"Yes, apologies. Taupe revolutionized neuroimaging by quantifying neurotransmitters using BRIAR software," she said, as an experienced Taupe student, quick on her feet.

"And, who did that?"

"Francesca Briar, my research mentor," Angel spoke to him directly, and in response, Dr. Pellin frowned and turned to his podium. "That was unfair, but yes, you are correct.

And, can somebody tell me how this ties into pharmacy… uh… Czerwonovsky.”

Even though Dr. Pellin mispronounced the name, Cupid stood up quickly, showing off his aquamarine outfit with its various necklaces, pearls, and gold accents.

“By understanding these brain chemicals, neurotransmitters, you can assess the pharmaceutical needs of the patient, case by case. In other words, you can carefully design a pill with manufacturing software, like BRIAR-M, simulate it among the human population with various statistical methods, and have a compliant, approved drug for individual use.” Cupid pushed up the reading glasses he was wearing, which he did not need.

“And, the difference between BRIAR-M and BRIAR? Let’s hear from…” Dr. Pellin looked down at the attendance sheet before Cupid interrupted him again, still standing.

“BRIAR-M gives you the exact compounds needed for the desired effect, whereas BRIAR is software solely used for imaging. It’s like… BRIAR-M tells you the recipe, but… BRIAR gives you a detailed image of the cake.”

“I mean, I’ve never heard that before, but… yes, very well said. Thank you.” Cupid sat down and tossed his hair in a small mirror. Angel and I looked at each other before I whispered in Slovak.

“When did you learn all that?”

“Oh, I just did the reading. Plus, I just see it as like… little colors and chemicals. Plus, BRIAR-M is kinda pretty.” Cupid beamed a smile and winked at me.

Angel scoffed in disbelief, and I sat back, stunned by the expertise that Cupid had. For a marketing major, he was at a PharmD student level in neurology. It took Angel two semesters to do basic BRIAR-M coding, and the fact that Cupid understood it in weeks festered an even stronger resentment in me. Once class ended, Dr. Pellin called Cupid to the front as Angel and I waited for him.

“Since when is your cousin, crazy Cupid, a genius?”

"I have no clue. He hated science growing up, so I'm just as shocked. He was a straight C student, and when my mother called me and told me about him attending Harlequin, I laughed." Although Harlequin looked for personality over intellect, they admitted students who had charm, energy, and tenacity. Taupe wanted brains, students who studied hard. Harlequin, on the other hand, networked hard. I'd heard rumors that they had bars where people did drugs, not drink. As the conversation was ending, Angel's phone buzzed, and she opened the Pallet Portal app. In the news section, which was monopolized by Harlequin personalities, there was one new story to be watched. It was a video of the boy who interviewed me, Tyle. His fingers were covered with rings, and he spoke in front of the Indigo campus, the twisted metal gates behind him.

"Everybody, hello. Indigo and Taupe face rising cases of BEV, a virus that causes the whites of the eyes to turn purple. The main symptom of these students has been coloration of the sahara… no, excuse me, the sclera. Or, whites of the eyes, making them look like a bruise. Symptoms include fever and fatigue, and little is known about the virus, only that it has origins in Dr. Freida Ilt's lab at Taupe University."

Angel turned to me while I rolled my eyes, and Cupid, who now stood behind me with an annoyed look on his face.

"I know it wasn't you. He just wants views, that's all. Somebody to blame, and being the only medical school…" Angel reassured me.

"Ugh, Tyle is an idiot," Cupid interrupted, motioning with his head to leave, as if he were the leader.

"You know him?" Angel asked, the video playing on loop on her phone.

"Yeah. He's this annoying freshman stealing stories from upperclassmen, just going to places. He has so much money, so he puts himself in things like this because he can."

Cupid spoke of Tyle like he was a mosquito. But Angel was right. They needed somebody to blame, somebody to take the fall. And, since Dr. Ilt did not inform us of the lab opening, I had no idea what was happening.

The next day, the story went viral and spread to all facets of school after multiple Harlequin students reported on it, making it hard to ignore. In the following days, Milena and Hawley sent a message to all Taupe faculty and students, encouraging masks and free tests. I looked at the image of the tests, with two lines that ran parallel to each other. It could tell you your cortisol level, and if there was the presence of the eye-altering pigments. They assured that nobody had died, and that you could monitor cases using a tracking portal. On the news, multiple companies and schools around the world noticed the colored eyes, with some offering therapy for free to compensate for the stress. In the information pamphlet, the Pallets provided to Taupe students, they outlined that Dr. Freida Ilt's lab has isolated the virus, working to create a vaccine, and is examining the exact location using global epidemiological case data. I shook my head in Angel's room. Since we did not isolate the virus, we weren't in the lab, and the global epidemiological data were from cities that were bombed with no survivors. It all wasn't true. I imagined Dr. Ilt was somewhere, shaking her head at what was happening. In class, she lectured as if all was normal, and interacted with me minimally. When a student asked about it, she said that she would maybe lecture on it toward the end of the year, time permitting, of course. Hours after class, I was sitting on Angel's plush comforter while I graded papers on a textbook.

"Did you get to his paper?" Angel spun around on her creaky chair. Pink glass, collectible butterflies decorated the top of her desk, alongside different types of vine plants in clay pots.

"No... right now it's some freshman... Nick... Nick Ameera. He's not bad, actually. He's making sense, unlike other people." I motioned to the stack of papers, the top one revealing an F with blocks of my small, green pen writing.

Angel walked to the bed, picked it up, and read it while I highlighted a sentence that made no sense on the next student's paper, before I noticed.

"Jesus…. you're ruthless. No wonder Paul's stressed." She walked around the room with the paper, my eyes fixated on it.

My head shot up. "Stressed? From this class?" She nodded.

"I mean, all the residents have it, I'm sure I have it. You have it. Did you guys see anything there, at Indigo?"

"I mean… they overwork them…"

"They overwork us, too," Angel remarked snidely.

I thought about what exactly made Indigo and Taupe different. All the students were overworked, yet Taupe wasn't nearly as affected. Maybe it was because our stress wasn't as acute, or maybe because it was anxiety of failure. Or, was it that Taupe was stressful and Indigo was traumatic? They had more severe cases due to a deeper-rooted fear. We were all afraid of grades, numbers that affected our hypothetical future in pharmaceutical companies. Indigo students were afraid to miss quotas, to have tangible evidence of their errors. Ours was at the subjective mercy of professors, of TAs. I didn't want to think about it, and luckily, Angel picked up Paul's paper to my annoyance to interrupt my overthinking.

"Put that back, Angel." I glared at her in a face that conveyed contempt. I did not want Dr. Ilt to have another reason to be mad at me, since I was on extremely thin ice.

"Fine… fine, Dr. Teddy Bear."

"I'm not a doctor… yet," I said flatly.

I hopped off the bed to use the bathroom, which was across the hall. Angel was a resident assistant on the floor below me, and the RA suites were single rooms. Not that Angel had many parties to break up, since the Pallet Ball dorm tower was on the opposite side of campus. But she got free tuition and free meals. Even in bed, I was chewing on an orange she stole on her weekly fruit heist from the dining hall. In the bathroom, I washed my hands with a small pebble of bar soap, drying them on a bleached towel that was once blue. It was the aftermath of the bleach party PBall threw last year. She had just started dating Paul and wanted to be there, but had nothing bleached.

Angel's eyes widened when I returned, to which I nodded politely back. For the next hour, I graded every paper on pox viruses, overall recognizing that the class was doing better than last time. However, about half outright failed, about a third barely passed, and the remainder got a B. It was better than the slaughter I did last week, far better than their first one, the tearful students, the twenty-eight students that dropped. I puffed air and stretched my arms above my head as I finished, and I slumped into Angel's bed.

"All set?" Angel said cheerfully.

"Yup… all set." I clicked my pen before stretching so hard my vision blurred.

"The ink massacre is over?"

"Yep… they did fine… wait." I flipped through the pile, realizing I had never seen Paul's paper.

"I must have missed Paul's…" I said, puzzled by my error.

"I thought you graded it before, right? That's what…" As Angel talked, I found a black and white paper with absolutely no notes in the center of the graded pile. All with the letter A at the top, and nothing close to my handwriting. I pulled it from the pile, examining it before looking at the nervous Angel.

"Did you…" My eyebrows furrowed, my eyes blinking at her.

"Listen, I…" she started to confess.

"Angel, come on. That's not cool at all." I shook my head, re-clicking the pen.

"Teddy, please. I know he's going to fail. And… the October game is already canceled, but…" she pleaded.

"The October Game is canceled? Wait, why?" I knew why, but I wanted to know what story was being told to PBall players.

"Indigo has been… well, you know, you saw it firsthand. They were supposed to host it, but canceled because they weren't ready. And you can't have a sport with only two teams, so…"

"So they bailed? When is the game, anyways?"

"In four weeks. But, Paul told me that…"

"Told you what?"

"They started expelling people who tested positive. People are saying they aren't going to have a season."

"Where did he hear this?" I wanted to understand what they were being told, because the reality of the outbreak preceded last week's game by a long time.

"All the Pallet players talk in the Portal, and multiple people heard it too. They said it ramped up after you left."

I could only imagine the reign of terror that Caelum and Claudia were causing. And since they had an all-or-nothing mentality, they paralyzed their student body with quotas for disobeying. I turned to Angel, frustrated and betrayed that she would try something behind my back.

"And so… Indigo not playing means you can… change your boyfriend's grade?"

"Because he wouldn't be able to play! He would only be a student and… they wouldn't curve it!" I knew they curved grades for PBall players, and I envisioned it was a conversation I would have with Dr. Ilt at the end of the semester. But for now, I had to be fair and hold Angel to that standard as well. I felt anger fester inside of me, due to the general anxiety, lack of sleep, and the virus that was not alleviating my stress at all.

"But what? You have to be the heroic… girlfriend to save him?" I lashed out at her.

"No… I…" Angel was starting to get shaky, while I didn't care. I continued to berate her.

"I could have gotten fired! Expelled! Dr. Ilt would have been the final nail in my coffin because, once again, I had a personal tie get in the way. Do not touch my work ever again. Not my grading, not anything else. You have absolutely no idea about what these papers are about." I raised my voice, suddenly infuriated. She stood there, wounded and tear-eyed.

"Just… please don't be so…" Her voice was shaky. I threw all the papers into my backpack, betrayed.

"I'm going. You have…" I looked up, and for the second I saw her, the whites of her eyes were purple. She stood there blinking for a moment, and with every blink, they darkened into a dark amethyst that almost made her eyes look black. I paused, looking at her angrily. She opened her mouth to try to apologize, her eyes black at this point. I saw the tearful eyes that stared at me at the funeral, softening only before I watched in horror as her legs gave out, her muscles became limp, and she collapsed to the floor. I had traumatized her, hit some sort of nerve that triggered something inside her.

"Angel!"

I rushed to her, throwing the papers on the ground. I slapped her face repeatedly and shook her shoulders. She wasn't breathing. After a few seconds, her eyes shot open, and she gasped for air. I was grateful I was the cure to this, but it confused Angel tremendously.

She opened her phone, which was on her desk, while I sat on the floor. I watched her check her eyes, now white, before turning to me.

"Wait a second… you… how did you do that? I felt like… you put my nerves to sleep."

"I… uh…" The room became silent as she stared at me, and I could feel my secret creep out of me.

"Did you… was…" With my eyes hot from embarrassment and shame, I looked at her.

"Oh my God, did you…"

"Angel, I didn't think it would start a whole…"

"Oh my God." She stormed out of her room as I got up. I explained to her how stressed I was, how tired I was, how it wasn't supposed to infect everybody. How I made the code not able to transmit, and how it became something bigger than me. How the doctoral spot was open, and I wanted to use it to get in.

"So you… make this thing which, mind you, was supposed to de-stress you. Instead, you made a virus that reacts to stress and trauma and…"

"Don't rub it in, please. I know."

"So… I just…" She slowly got herself up, with her eyes being a sick, poisonous frog blue. "Just go. I don't want to fight and… clearly neither does my body. This is a lot to… handle for me. I'm sorry I tried to change his grade… just be easy on him, okay?"

I sat outside the Immunology Building after shamefully storming out of Angel's room, watching people move in and out. I felt slightly relieved, but more so overwhelmed and seething with mistrust. Who would Angel tell? Did she really have my back, or run to her boyfriend? On the bench, I watched students in masks and lab coats come and go. Some of the students I noticed had colored sclera, others held up mirrors and pulled at their eye bags. It was truly everywhere, and something that we seemed fairly unfazed by. This stress virus was now normalized, almost expected. With Dr. Ilt's lab closed, the other nine immunology labs were likely working hard, collaborating, and putting us to shame. The neurology labs would figure out a way to profit from it, and a focus on managing stress would be the latest craze. I thought that there were immunology labs that isolated the virus, aside from Peter Cheshire-Yu, and they were probably running safety tests in ILLUMAKE to make sure the vaccine would work. Vaccines would roll out next week, this crisis would be averted, and who knows what would happen to me, my work, or even Dr. Ilt's PharmD cohort. Everything could implode because of me, and my desire to be immune to stress. I took a drag of my cigarette as a man in a mask sat next to me, irritating me as I glared at him.

"Can I—" the man asked.

"No," I interrupted bitterly.

I was in no mood to share, let alone talk to anybody. He proceeded to sit next to me, much to my general irritation. I was more shocked at his complete disregard, but also the green corduroy suit he wore.

"That's a shame…" The person removed his mask to reveal Filmore Pallet. I sat, confused as to why the president of Harlequin was sitting here. His eyes, behind gold glasses, were bright green and bright blue. When a pack of students walked by, all wearing masks, he inched away from me.

"I know I'm infected, you are too. Just gotta…" He mockingly meditated, which made me smirk. "Keep calm. So, would it be possible NOW for me to have a smoke?"

I passed him a cigarette and a lighter, the two of us sitting there.

"I'm glad I ran into you," he muttered, after puffing smoke. We took drags in between talking.

"Why is that, to tell me how my lab caused this mess?"

"No… frankly, to warn you."

"Warn me?" My spine stiffened, and I pushed back my glasses.

Filmore sighed, rubbing his hands together as he placed the cigarette in his mouth. It rested on his lip as he spoke. "They know you did it, they know that… you were the leak. They know you made it." Filmore's tone was no longer comfortable, and I became even more aware of his old age when he talked. Being defensive was the only way I knew to deflect this.

"And… no, you're wrong." I stood up, offended by the accusation that was entirely true.

I looked around, making sure that Dr. Ilt or anybody else wasn't hearing this. The pine trees swaying in the wind, students with colored sclera rushing. Filmore, once the jolly and aloof president, now seemed condescending. Once jolly was now large, old was now creepy.

"I'm not wrong… and you know that I'm not. But this isn't a gotcha moment, or a… confess up. That wouldn't do anything."

I studied his face wrinkles, his smile lines, and the baseball hat with a neon green jester stamped on. "So… what do you…?" I asked, more irritated by the constant amorphous punishments. Between Caelum and Claudia's military persona, to Dr. Ilt expelling me, to the Pallets now knowing what I did, I felt decision paralysis. Where I tried to gain control of myself, I was starting to feel less control, as the days went on.

"I'll fill you in on a secret." Filmore flicked the cigarette, bouncing on the smooth limestone pathway. "They are struggling with it, this virus you made." Filmore coughed before continuing, "You were the only person here… who had the balls to use a bioweapon on yourself. And well, they can't find anything for a cure, or a vaccine." Filmore nodded at somebody who walked by, continuing in a low voice. "Now… I recommend… you either make the vaccine before another lab does, or at least present your understanding of it."

"Or?" I interrupted impatiently.

"Lose to Mark. They like his… confidence," Filmore said, flatly.

"Why don't they… blame me? Expose me?"

"Because to expose you would mean that you weren't controlled. By saying 'Teddy and His Virus!' they would have to admit that you were… out of their bounds. That you were…"

"Smarter than them." I coughed smoke, something I haven't done in almost a decade with my first cigarette.

"Exactly. And… I'm here to warn you, exactly that. You are smarter than they are. They know that, and it's time you knew that."

The oldest Pallet sibling warning me was unsettling; it felt strange, only because I barely knew Filmore. Was he an ally? A friend? Therefore, it was weirder when he grabbed my glasses off my face, while I was too stunned.

"Pallet glass, indestructible and tough," He joked like an advertiser as I asked for my glasses back. When he refused, he promised there was a point.

"Now, that itself is a myth. Indestructible," he said, banging them loudly on the metal part of the bench. When nothing happened, he turned to me. "But, the secret is… everything can be destroyed."

He flipped his hand, with the Pallet glass ring on the middle finger, and punched down swiftly on the bridge of my glasses. Immediately, both his ring and my glasses turned into a soft dust, some of which was carried in the wind, some in his hand. I stared at the powder that was my glasses, and looked up as Filmore stretched his back.

"Time to get new glasses, Teddy."

As he walked away, his blurry silhouette disappeared among the crowd. I looked down at the powder, and I realized why it looked so familiar. It was the same powder as Indigo's side of the Pallet Ball field.

Chapter Eight

I was about six years old when, one day, I started to have a low-grade fever. My mother kept me home from school the next day, but when I started to cough and my fever persisted, the circumstances got more dire. I remember going in and out of states of delirium, my mother standing with me in the ice-cold shower to rinse the sweat off. After about three days, we visited the doctor, who determined I must have had some sort of viral pneumonia. They said to get plenty of rest, drink plenty of fluids, and my mother was the most frustrated. She was so bitter, claiming that they did absolutely nothing and that claiming it's a virus is a doctor's laziness and inability to do their job.

The next day, when it was harder to wake up, I slept for about sixteen hours. Sweating profusely, I remember seeing my father check my temperature with a glass thermometer. Being hoisted once again by my father, I was driven to the hospital, not the doctor's office. My eyes had become a shade of dandelion yellow that my father only saw with his dying father, who was an alcoholic. I remember my father carrying me, after my mother helped me change into a hospital gown with tears in her ink-blue eyes. For the next few hours, immunologists and various experts gave detailed hypotheses about what was happening, why I was yellow, and why I took so long to get better. I learned all this when I was in high school, but apparently, my parents got into such a bitter argument that it was interrupted by an immunologist, one who had a promising treatment for me.

It was from the United States, and my data was sent to the Pallet family for consultation. My mother recounted to me that, as they waited for the drug to work, my father had to hold her back from verbally assaulting the doctors. That they were being reckless and stupid, and my father defended them until I sat up in my bed without help. It was as if they put a special cleaning agent in my veins that, with every heartbeat, I could feel it progressively battle whatever was inside me. The dreadful aches, the coughing fits, all seemed to vanish in a matter of twenty minutes. I cried when I hugged my mom, feeling her tears on my back as her wedding ring pressed into the soaked gown.

When I got home, we had a light dinner of venison soup, which my mother assured me I should eat as much as possible. "So…" I started, with a groggy and parched voice. The only light in my kitchen was above the pot of soup on the stove and the humble wooden table.

"Yes?" My father looked at me from his bowl, which he was drinking out of. My mother elegantly sipped the soup with a spoon, her hair in a bun.

"Why… was I so sick? Was it the flu?" I asked, recounting that last year I had the flu for about a week with similar symptoms. My parents shot each other a glance, which I noticed.

"It wasn't the flu like… last year, sweetheart. But… it was a… worse flu." My mother said.

"A worse flu? How is that… possible?"

"Well…" My father cleared his throat before wiping the broth on his lips with the napkin.

"You know how your aunt and uncle work with… defending this country?" my father said, pushing his empty clay bowl on the salmon, woven table mat.

"Gregor…" My mom stopped him, tired of the countless doctor talk. My mother also hated talking about the ammunition factory when I was a kid, considering it was making bullets after all.

"Well, they make sure that nothing happens to us, nothing bad happens to this country, right?"

I nodded, blinking as I chewed my meal.

"See, your body is the same. There are tiny… factories and soldiers that fight to keep bad stuff out."

"Like the flu!" I exclaimed.

"Exactly, like the flu. The flu is a bad guy that… weakens… no, what's a better word… um…" My father looked up and snapped his fingers.

"Beat up your soldiers," my mother added.

My father smiled at my mother, who returned gently. "Yes, exactly, exactly what your mother said. The flu beats up your tiny little soldiers in your body and…you feel sick."

"But…" I pondered, confused. "What about this time? It wasn't the flu?"

My father inhaled and drank from his beer bottle.

"No… it was a very bad flu." My mother fluttered her ink-blue eyes, clearly masking the distress the past few weeks had caused. "And we are glad that… you are better, because it was an awful… virus," my mother added.

For the next few days, I proceed to bullet them with questions about immunology, about the soldiers, about the factories in my body. My mother, at one point, got irritated at my Socratic questioning and snapped at me in the car driving to school. Still, the concept of something completely draining me, making my eyes yellow, was something that drew me in. I often cite being sick as the "Why," and brought it up on my application to Taupe. It was the salient reason that I was pursuing immunology.

By the time I was applying to college, I had already worked at the Department of Infectious Disease Control and done countless research essays on everything you could. If I wasn't writing essays, I was embroidering. By the time I arrived at Taupe, the first-semester courses were a breeze. But once everybody was on the same playing field, then they really increased the workload, and Dr. Ilt scouted me. Even then, I had never thought that I would be put on a train to a Pallet School and tasked with solving an outbreak.

Back in my room, my gray-toned sanctuary, I found my way to the box of memories without my glasses in the corner. With my desk lamp and overhead light, I found my way to the box. Somehow, I knew that what I was looking for would be in there. I was lucky that I was farsighted, because I could barely make out the photos, the documents, and the DVD's from the box. I held up my mother's medical school diploma, with my father's finance degree. I placed them gingerly on the desk and found an old, dark oak jewelry box with other items in it.

It was the box on my dad's dresser, which held family heirlooms that preceded me. His father's watch, a couple of rings, and what I was searching for. His boxy, thin metal-framed glasses. When I put them on, they were much lighter than my old pair and took some adjusting. But my father would constantly lose and find his glasses, and had them scattered around the house in various locations. Now, I was lucky that he had a pair in the box, lucky that he was so predictable even when he wasn't here.

The next few days, Pallet Portal messages from journalists flooded my inbox. People asking for a quote or expert insight, since I was apparently an expert from my Indigo panel. I threw my phone on the bed and zipped my backpack, ready to start the usual day. The thought of Dr. Pellin's class made me groan as I made my bed. I would be getting more papers to grade by tonight at midnight, and would have to have them done as soon as possible. The lab was still closed, and there were rumors I heard from around the dining hall of one lab, Alten's lab, that was close to developing a vaccine that worked on most patients. It made little sense to me as to how, since every virus mutated so dramatically.

Sliding on deodorant, a Portal message from Dr. Pellin threw me off completely, one that claimed we had a surprise presentation. What would make me anxious or even excited now didn't faze me. With new events, people, and change happening, I couldn't care less. I had become so apathetic, so bored with everything. After eating breakfast alone, I made my way to the Neurology Building. I said good morning to nobody, put my hands in my hoodie, and kept my head down as always. Angel didn't text, and I didn't text her. I opened the door, sitting in the first seat I saw that was open and near the door.

In a blood red suit, a pearly white button-up, and six-inch black stilettos, Cupid walked around the classroom responding to a compliment by some girl in the front row, who was Moxy. Now mildly intrigued, I made my way to my usual seat, intending to ask Cupid what was going on. I couldn't see Angel, so I sat in the front. That was when Dr. Pellin introduced Cupid and the project he had been working on for the past few weeks.

As Dr. Pellin spoke, Cupid passed out candy hearts to the front row, something he did even in high school when he ran for student government. On top of that, he brought donuts and coffee for the class, and he urged people to get up at any point to get refreshments in the back. Dr. Pellin gave Cupid the microphone while my eye twitched, who grabbed it with long, pearly colored fingernails.

"Good morning, everybody! My name is Cupid Czerwonovsky, a graduating senior at Harlequin. I promise I won't be bitter toward you for beating us at the Pallet Ball game. I'll let that go."

The class purred with light laughter; it was the standard number of people today. He seemed to be charged by them; with every person he made eye contact with, he sounded more certain, more direct. It was the first time I had seen Cupid give an academic talk, or any public speech for that matter, aside from charismatic toasts at Easter lunches. My jealousy was fueled by not only his presentation skills, but the delicious raspberry donut I sank my teeth into. "Today, I will be discussing the work that I completed with Dr. Pellin in his lab. Together, we created this little guy. We call it... limerzine. In brief, it is a pill that, once taken, will make the patient fall in love with the first person they see. In science terminology, it releases dopamine, oxytocin, adrenaline, and noradrenaline acutely upon certain perception triggers. We designed it for those who are struggling to get pregnant or… frankly… those couples with intimacy problems. It lasts about ten hours and resets in the patient's sleep with one circadian rhythm cycle. Let's get started."

He held up a small, pink colored pill that looked like a shrunken Pallet Ball. My jaw dropped when he revealed it.

Throughout the entire presentation, I sat amazed by his intelligence. He navigated questions expertly, from neurology majors who do similar work to Dr. Pellin. How could someone like him, with little science background, have this accomplishment? I definitely decided that this must have been Dr. Pellin's work, and Cupid was taking the credit. Still, even if that was the case, the grimace on my face could not hide the fact that he could charm his way into a school, put himself in a lab for fun, and steal their credit. When he concluded forty minutes later, I asked the last question. He smiled and gestured to me, and I asked with the tone of Dr. Ilt.

"So, Cupid, I understand you study branding. What made you want to come here and take this class?"

"That's a great question…" Cupid started.

"English, please, you two!" Dr. Pellin shouted from the back of the class. We always default to Slovak, but it was hard not to. We nodded in acknowledgment and repeated ourselves. Cupid circled the center of the classroom, not wobbling or struggling to walk in the skinny heels.

"It's because… understanding the way people think, and how their choices are to be made. If I am studying branding, which I am, not stealing your jobs, I want to be able to… understand my client as much as possible. If I need to… make a sale or market something… I want to understand the chemistry of how they think, how they feel. Not to… manipulate them… but to tailor how I talk, how I… present. And, lab work like this… I can now say I did it. And, well… I always found mental health interesting. It kinda… clicks for me. And now that I have the time… and mental space to study it, I want to take advantage fully. I hope that answered your question."

"I see. You did, thank you." I sat back, impressed.

"And, what isn't as obvious, is I now understand what it takes to have a lab, to produce these treatments. It really broadens what I can sell, what I can… develop in the future."

The polished nature of his response was razor sharp and right. People concurred and nodded, giving him a round of applause. I knew exactly why he made it. He couldn't care less about any sort of couple, any sort of fertility. He wanted it for himself, to make anybody fall in love with him chemically. My jealousy stewed a little longer as I put my stuff away. It was better than my circumstances, since he could actively control it. He could give anybody the pill; he could even drug them. Now, Cupid could control people's infatuation, people's adoration of him.

After Cupid's performance, I went to Khill. I would normally have work, but right now I could get ahead on grading. In the brightly lit corridor with arched, ancient wood, I stood still as I watched Angel, seemingly back to normal, sort stacks of books, with her eyes dark blue. From yards away, I could tell that she was stressed. Her forehead was clammy; I could see she was sick, not allowing herself to succumb.

"Angel… stop. ANGEL," I raised my voice and rushed to her, to which she looked at me in annoyance.

There were students sitting at the tables behind us, turning their heads, but I was indifferent. Angel mattered more to me than a stranger's grade.

"Can't talk, Teddy," she said, placing a parasite textbook onto a cart. I understood why she would be bitter at me, but I still cared for her.

I tried to speak in a hushed whisper, with students around me still staring, "You have to stop, your eyes are…"

"Yeah, yeah. I know they are, I know. BEV. But, I have to do this." She held another, larger textbook. I could see sweat glistening from her head, and I tried to intervene by standing in front of the book cart.

"Angel, no, stop it." I tried to take the book from her, but she slapped my hand. Her eyes didn't change at all, and I pulled away, puzzled. "What is going on with you? I have work I need to… and you said yourself: 'Do not mess with my work.'" Her eyes were the exact same shade of blue, maybe slightly darker.

"How are you still…" I whispered to myself in disbelief that somebody with sclera so dark was able to be upright for so long. "Angel, just take a break, I can pay you the…"

"No, you are not paying me shit, and no, I can't take a break! Don't you get it! I can't, not at all! I have to sort these books, I have to… Jesus! You can't cure me or be glued to me all the time! I have to sort these fucking stupid books, and then study, and then read, and then make sure that… none of your students want to die, and then make sure Paul is okay, and then make sure YOU are okay…" She inhaled a breath before turning to me, with a textbook in her hand.

"It's a lot. It's stressful, but… it's my life. I'm at peace with it. And you can't help me."

The fact that her body was still functional, still able to move, must have been due to her understanding of what made her stressed. What exactly made her cortisol spike? I watched her file books onto a cart and push past me bitterly.

I followed her. "Angel… you need to rest."

"I told you, I can't. Let me do my job… and I'll let you do yours."

"That's what this is about?"

"Yes, Teddy, it is. I'm pissed at how… harsh you are, how you graded him, and that we're in this mess… with these eyes… in the first place."

"Angel, that has nothing to do with you. See, you think you can just… coddle him, you can…"

"No, I never said that. But, Jesus, Teddy, just because you're the TA and work for her doesn't mean that you can be a dick. Or, abuse your power and make something like that."

"I'm not being a dick to him! I'm being… I'm grading how I'm expected."

"Well… it's fucked up, and you stress the freshmen out, too. This entire fucking school… lives off it. Either stress from… lab work or… library work, or schoolwork. It… fucking keeps the lights on."

Angel parted two books and slid a heavy red one in between them, checking something on a list. Above us, painted portraits of the Pallet siblings stared down at us. Filmore holding a book, smiling, Milena standing over a desk, and Hawley sitting on a gold-accented chair. I couldn't look Angel in the eyes, furious and guilty about the illness she had, a cocktail of emotions that I hated. A student came up to her and asked if we could be quiet, which she apologized for before turning to me, without making eye contact.

"Listen… just… go easy on them. Not just Paul, but…the last thing we need is another thing against us, failing us. Or, making us sicker. I have to get back to the desk but… yeah."

As if she had more to say, she pushed the cart on the dark wooden floor, causing some squeaks. Feeling dismissed, I walked past the old shelves of modern, shiny books, while thinking about what Angel told me.

I had never been asked for academic mercy, and I always seemed to push harder when it got hard. I would remind myself of that and everything my parents had to do. My mother became a woman surgeon in Slovakia, and my father managed the hospital's finances. Now, with Angel upset at me and my parents gone, I realized how isolated I was. Before I was about to leave, a singular book caught my eye. As I approached it, I realized that it would take all night to understand its contents, if not more. It would be a start, and would consume me. After reading the first few chapters, I decided it had the information I needed in order to truly understand my virus. I slid it into my bag, and as I walked through the vast study section, I made my way to Angel's desk with an even wilder thought. At the dark wooden help desk, Angel was writing a book location for a student on a small piece of paper.

"Yeah, so it'll be between BRIAR coding books and general behavioral neurology, okay?" I expected the student to be afraid of Angel, but turned around to have slightly green-tinted sclera. She ignored me as she typed.

"Hello, how can I help you?" she said, performatively.

"I need a six," I said confidently.

"Six what?" she said, not turning her head from the computer.

"Six-sided keyboard. A Hexboard," I asked, in a low voice.

Angel put her elbow on the table and turned her body, giving me a look at how stupid the request was.

"You don't have access to that..." She was right, since only PharmD students could get them from the library.

"I don't care, I need it, I need it to... code this vaccine."

Angel put her tongue in her cheek, shaking her head. "You really just... want to fuck up everybody's life, huh? Mine, Paul's, and all your students. Teddy, I could lose my job."

The blue in her eyes darkened slightly, and I breathed a shaky sigh.

"Angel, listen to me. I..." I started to sound frantic, speaking quickly as if it were a conspiracy.

Angel pressed her chipped nail on a scanning gun, matching the LED light. I could tell she was not going to budge even before she spoke, "I'm not going to, Teddy. You don't know six-sided coding at all, and I can't let you do that."

Seeing Angel working while infected led me to one thought: there had to be something in the viral code that was person-specific. I had to find out what made it different, and why. I thought about Lee and how he had to sit down after being overworked at the factory. Angel didn't seem to slow down at all, and she seemed even more motivated to work.

The cold air harshly hit my face as I sped down the main pathway, gunning for Dr. Ilt's lab. I wasn't supposed to go there, but Filmore telling me that the Pallets were watching me gave me a sort of invincibility. That the Pallets could be in the lab and watch me enter, and do nothing about it.

"Teddy!" Cupid's voice boomed across campus. He made no effort to run to me, and I was focused on deciphering the BEV code.

"Hi Cupid, listen, I have to… whoa…" The whites of his eyes were a swirl of purple and green, and he talked at a slower pace. Sweat glistened on his forehead.

"Yeah, so um… I got inked! I tried to call you but…"

"It's fine. How are you feeling?"

"I feel fine, and this happened like… ten minutes ago. I don't know what to do, or like… what it is."

"Look, Cupid, just… get some rest. Do you know what's stressing you?"

"Stressing me? God no! The reasons that stress me out… well… they're in the ground. Besides, what are you doing about it?"

"The outbreak? I mean… I was going to go right now…"

"Can I come? I mean, I can show you Pellin's lab…"

My first instinct was to lie to Cupid, say I had grading (which, I still did). But, on second thought, I needed somebody to compare with, to see if there was any difference in the viral code of different people from different Pallet Schools. After hearing about Cupid's afternoon shopping, going on a date, and talking to his cousins, I keyed into the lab that had the lights on. My heart sank with anxiety, and I slowly entered the hall. I expected to see Dr. Ilt typing in her office, and had the dreadful thought of seeing Mark. Yet, it was somebody who was dusting the computers and gave a polite nod in acknowledgment before exiting.

"Sit down here." I pointed to my desk chair as Cupid stood with his arms crossed.

"And do what?"

"I have… a hunch about this virus, because I think it's host-specific in its severity that's based on school… and I want you…" I logged into my computer, not looking at Cupid opening a bag of chips.

"To be your amazing, wonderful, incredible, drop-dead gorgeous lab rat." He tossed his hair and pouted his lips.

"Sure," I said, not humoring him at all.

I grabbed a blood vial and lancet, holding out my hand as he batted his eyes at me.

"Will it hurt?"

"No, it'll tickle," I retorted to the stupid question.

He snickered as I warned of a small pinch on his finger. Once the small vial was full of blood, I gave Cupid a pink Band-Aid and walked it over to the ILLUMAKE machine. I clicked the blood into the back of the machine and checked the computer, as the initial blood analysis was starting. I weaved through blocks of data, told Cupid his iron was low, but got to the main report of the viruses in his blood. I went through a list of various benign viruses and found one that shared the same profile as the one I designed. It was chilling to see it in your cousin's blood, but ethics were not the main focus right now. When I clicked the full viral code, it was roughly 52,000 different lines. I scanned all of the letters and scrolled, not sure what I was looking for. I scrolled for about a minute, aimlessly. Perhaps a clue on how the virus worked, or how it treated cortisol. Did it raise it? Did it eat it? Did it mutate in Cupid? Cupid was eating a bag of chips over my shoulder, crunching right near my ear.

"This looks… fucking disgusting," Cupid mumbled over chips.

"Didn't you have to do this for your pill? In Pellin's lab?" I said, tossing through the textbook I stole from Khill. It was advanced viral coding techniques by Peter Cheshire-Yu, which were proving not to be effective. I was hoping the pharmaceutical software BRIAR was similar in its coding complexity, and kept asking Cupid for help. When he showed it to me for his pill, it looked nothing like ILLUMAKE, with far more panels and graphics than simple code.

"Hell no... we just have a computer program do the whole thing. We run it, see what we like and don't, sometimes edit, but other times... it's pretty easy to make. Then, we monitor the mice, and if that works, then... well, trials. So... really, anybody could make a pill. About anything. I'm pretty sure there's some labs making a stress reducer for this virus thing, so people can calm down and not have... inky eyes."

My eyes twitched as I realized how easy it could have been to make a pill for my stress, and not start a pandemic.

"I mean... yeah. It's why all the line bars at Quinn are running. They all have older PHARMAKE machines with pre-set drug recipes. They just don't do trials or mice, they just use humans... their clients... ooh!" Cupid touched my screen with his greasy finger on a line of Cyrillic and Chinese characters seemingly woven together.

"That's cool, I know that. And... weirdly... enough... scroll a second." Cupid hiccuped and covered his mouth with his fist before I watched him squint at the screen. His breath smelled like barbecue chips, and the crunching was getting on my nerves. I hadn't noticed how muscular he was, but being at eye level to his shoulders and neck made it glaringly obvious.

"Right... here! This... this spells out... king... no... wait... court?" I could tell that Cupid was puzzled, trying to figure out what he was seeing, noticing a pattern in the code. Every so often, the genetic codes would spell funny words, but I could imagine it would be more complex if you had over 50,000 letters. The likelihood of words being spelled increases dramatically.

"Hm… it spells cortisol in Ukrainian," Cupid said flatly.

He ended up scribbling Ukrainian letters right next to me on a legal pad he found on a neighboring desk. I blinked at him before looking at the code closely. That was a weird coincidence, the letters spelling cortisol. But they weren't together, and they were separated by the same four Chinese characters. I wanted to see something and see if there was some sort of overlap. I plunged a lancet into my finger without flinching, which Cupid watched in shock.

"Oh my God… are you a machine?"

"No… it's just a small pinch, that's all."

I milked blood out of my thumb into the vial, holding it. I licked the small drop of blood coming out of the cut and went to the supply room. The lights turned on with motion, and I threw a scoop of ice into a Styrofoam bowl. When I returned to the station, I unclicked Cupid's blood from the machine and ignored the "DISCARD IN BIOHAZARD" banner that came on the screen. I didn't know if I needed to reuse it, so I placed it in the ice. After running my code, I could see that my viral code had many more complicated characters. Side by side, I noted how different the first 100 lines were. I found the entire line that Cupid said spelled cortisol in Ukrainian, my leg bouncing in anticipation as I waited for the program to load.

My heart sank when it said there weren't any matches. Deeply sighing, Cupid noticed and walked over.

"Nothing?"

"Yeah… nothing. It's fine…"

"Good guess about the Ukrainian thing, it's weird how it was separated by those… Chinese… Korean… I don't know… those symbols."

"They were Chinese," I added, deleting the last Ukrainian letter and looking at the four Chinese characters.

"Do me a favor, Cupid. Pull up translate and… wait, never mind."

Yawning loudly, I searched for the Chinese characters in my code. And there, in my code, it appeared two times. My eyes bulged as my neck craned toward the screen in suspicion. In line 29,827, there was a character in between two letters: R and T. It wasn't until I went to the next line of those Chinese characters that my heart truly sank, as I saw one word broken up again. When I removed all the Chinese characters in line 29,827, the Slovak word for the stress hormone remained: KORTIZOL. One line, 49,108 of my virus's genetic code, when all the Chinese characters were removed, one word remained.

RUŠTINA.

The Slovak word for Russian.

"Oh my GOD!" I stood up from my chair, shaking my head and pacing. I felt exposed and violated, like somebody had peered into my mind through viral genetic code.

"What? What? What? What's the matter?" Cupid frantically came to me as I paced back and forth.

"Holy shit… Cupid, this is fucked. Like, really fucked." I was speaking fast, trying to wrap my head around it.

"What's fucked? What is it?"

"The virus. It's host-specific. It adapts to your stress in your language and what raises your cortisol. That's why it's a different virus, because every person has a different stressor and a different language. Mine is Russian. I'm so… fucking afraid that they're going to… bomb us that… the language everything… holy shit."

"So… wait, slow down. Stop… Teddy… your eyes… STOP!" Cupid grabbed my shoulder, forcibly grounding me.

"How does that even work?" Cupid insisted.

"I don't know. This is weird. This is REALLY fucking weird."

When he released me, I was speed walking laps around the desks, Cupid shaking his head in disbelief, the only light in the lab was from the computer. He was looking at the code, making noises of disbelief as I finally cooled down.

"This is insane. Do the Pallets… know this? This could solve everything, can't you make some kind of… vaccine with this?" Cupid was asking questions that were logical, but I was emotionally spiraling.

"I don't know… I really don't know…"

When Cupid asked to check his blood, I typed with my hand shaking. I didn't even want to know; I felt like this was grotesquely personal. I shouldn't know what his deepest stressors are, but he insisted. I thought about anybody who gave their blood to the Pallets, for this new test I designed, or even checking their vitamin levels. They could, now, because of me, find a way to control them. To know what stressed them the most. When I searched for the characters, I stood up and walked away.

"What are you doing?" Cupid was licking the crumbs off his fingers, the bright glow hitting his smooth, moisturized face.

"I'm not… doing this. I can't do this, Cupid. This is wrong… just… look. And find it."

Cupid scanned the screen and inhaled, scrolling and clicking quickly.

"Did you find it?" I asked, standing in front of Dr. Ilt's door.

"Yes, I did," Cupid said, suddenly quiet and reserved.

"Well… what does it say? You don't have to…"

Cupid then went to his legal pad to write. It dawned on me, looking over his shoulder, that the line of code wasn't the same at all. His stress line wasn't in Slovak. When he was finished, he stared blankly at the paper, motionless. It was in the Russian alphabet.

"What is it? What does that mean? Isn't that… Russian?" I asked him.

"It means Ukrainian and… no… it's in Ukrainian, not Russian," he said somberly.

We sat in the chairs, hearing only our shallow breathing and the clock ticking.

"So… this virus… mutates to… not only the person, but their language?" Cupid muttered, staring into space.

"Yes. That's right," I whispered, as a tear rolled down my cheek.

I pulled the folder from Indigo out of my bag, with the countless tables and useless information. In the massive packet with all the people, the column wasn't virus identification codes; it was where the stressor was genetically written. The first patient's stressor was on line 19164, another student's 10167, and Cupid's stressor line on 25082. My stressor in my body was in the Latin alphabet, with Cupid's stress coded in his body in the Ukrainian, Cyrillic alphabet.

Cupid puffed air at me before rising and telling me, "You need a vacation."

"Tell me about it," I said, with my eyes closed and my head tilted upward. The number of life-altering events that happened in the past weeks felt crushing, and the speed at which this outbreak was spreading overwhelmed me. I felt like Mark, Dr. Ilt, and the Pallets all wanted to take me down for different reasons. Cupid rubbed my tense shoulder in an attempt to be supportive.

"No, no, seriously. You need to get out of here…"

"And where?"

I knew after I asked what Cupid wanted, and his grin confirmed that. Normally, when I got overwhelmed with school, I would fly home for the weekend. But that was no longer possible, and going to New York made more sense beyond just a vacation. Since I helped the outbreak thus far, understanding Taupe and narrowing down the virus, to introducing the test to Indigo, there was one last school to secure and make sure the Pallets, and Dr. Ilt, knew that I was serious. To be able to present observational findings on all three universities would be ideal, but I thought even more about it. It was risky, but at this point, they were already considering Mark.

After ironing out logistics, I shut off the computer, discarded the blood in the biohazard bin, and made arrangements to take the Friday train to New York City to visit not only Harlequin University but also Dr. Peter Cheshire-Yu. If I were going to get this spot, I wanted to understand everything about BEV.

Chapter Nine

The train ride from Hartford to New York City was a mix of talking to Cupid, reading, and planning the conversation with Dr. Cheshire-Yu. As I packed, I found his gold business card and confirmed that his lab was in New York City, and proceeded to email him. I specified that I had questions regarding immunology, his approach to data collection and analysis for flu patients, and would explore other topics as they arise. I sent the email yesterday, and didn't want to think about it too much.

I was answering a set of questions from a Pellin reading on reward systems in the brain, which Cupid had already done, and offered his answers. I was curious to see what Harlequin was like and get a sense for how it could be better suited for the stress outbreak. Now that I knew it was individual, it was a matter of how the environment made the stressors. In other words, the goal was to find the most common stressor at Harlequin. If academics were Taupe's and meeting quotas was the stressor at Indigo, what made Harlequin have blue eyes? I had so many questions that I could finally have answered: was it stress or trauma? Was I an exception? These were all questions that I jotted down in a notebook as Cupid and I spoke together. We were speaking Slovak when somebody got off at Bridgeport, extremely skinny, and wore green cargo shorts. His pale skin looked like a lizard's, with a smoker's voice.

"Y'all sound like Nazis, you know that?"

We just blinked at him, Cupid having some sort of powder puff in his hand. I was frozen and didn't want another verbal assault to come on. I was glad I was between the man and Cupid, knowing the temper tantrums I would see growing up.

Cupid was mid-powder application and cheerfully replied, "Oh… well… sorry about that." He sounded exactly like his mother. Cool and pointed.

"Yeah… whatever. Queers," he murmured when he shuffled past our seats, where I sat frozen.

"Why did you say that? Like… why did you give him the power?" I was speaking English to Cupid, afraid that there would be somebody else.

"Oh, sweetheart. He was close enough; I didn't want to give him a history lesson on Tiso. Besides, if he said Russian, then that would be a problem." He poked at me, and I let out air through my nostrils as a laugh, which he noticed. He continued pressing white powder under his eyes, staring into a compact.

"I mean… I'm used to it. Hell, I've been told I sound like I'm casting spells when I speak it. I'm not going to NOT use it. I mean… I really only talk to you, not my other cousins… except Arty and sometimes Rosy."

Cupid's dad had two older siblings, making Cupid have a total of four cousins who all spoke Ukrainian with one another. Arty and Rosy, however, spoke Czech sometimes because of their mother and the fact that they lived in Prague. At the funeral of Cupid's parents, I remember hugging Daria and Peter and trying my hardest to give them condolences in Ukrainian. It was slightly awkward, but I was relieved when Arty and Rosy showed up so I could speak Slovak freely.

"How are you doing?" I asked Cupid, turning my body toward him.

It was the first time I felt genuinely comfortable opening up to Cupid after the bombing, not full of the mistrust I harbored before. I asked him and closed my laptop; it was about to die anyway, and the questions for Pellin's class weren't as overwhelming as last week's.

"I'm uh… I'm all right. It really hasn't hit me that… you know. She's not coming back. I won't hear her again. That… when…" A tear went down Cupid's face.

I was frozen, afraid. I felt like I was watching a celebrity break down and cry. I hadn't seen him cry since the funeral. Besides, he still looked angelic when he cried. "But hey, you know. Avana didn't raise a bitch, and I'm not gonna change the world over a box of tissues."

He wiped his tears as he continued, "I knew that I wasn't going to heal by staying there, so... I had to start fresh here, and so I bought a new apartment with the money. Did some shopping, went to a really fucking expensive salon."

He tossed his hair, pulling up his bouncing peppermint colored curls.

"I always meant to ask…why the red and white?"

"Oh, well, at certain angles, the red looks like little hearts. It's based on my curl pattern." He turned his head, and I counted three heart-shaped marks on his head. Cupid jumped back into the conversation about Harlequin.

"And besides, marketing and branding aren't hard at all, really. You just have to… you know… bullshit half the time. It's just… poetic and sparkly lying, honestly."

On my phone, it notified me of a new email from Peter Cheshire-Yu.

Teddy,
Great to hear from you.
Let's do the main office at three. I'll have Ki let you up.
12 West 74th Street.
Welcome to New York.
Cheers,
Peter

My heart rippled in my chest, and when Cupid asked who was emailing me, I said it was work stuff. Which, it technically was. I told Cupid I had a meeting with a company at three, which one I didn't specify, nor did he ask. As soon as we got off the train, we walked a couple of blocks in what I assumed to be the direction of Harlequin. I could see a tall, glistening structure in the distance when a voice called behind us. Cupid was going to give me a tour, then Hampton and the green-haired boy seemingly materialized closer behind us.

"Q! Q!" they shouted. "Oh… Hammy! Froggy, hi! I'm just giving Teddy a tour of Quinn."

Cupid's English-speaking voice was performative and high-pitched, enforcing who exactly he was at this school. The socialite, the celebrity. No longer the crying, puffy-faced cousin.

As we walked, it turned out that Hammy was Cupid's first-year roommate, and Froggy was somebody they met last year at Lulu's Line Bar, which apparently sold lines of drugs as well as alcohol. Cupid and Froggy only kissed twice, and apparently spit sisters four times over. I didn't understand what they meant by that, but I could fill in the gaps as I marveled at Harlequin's campus from the outside.

There was a massive, gleaming glass arched bridge that I could not take my eyes off. There were people standing on it, yet it seemed like it connected two buildings, which I instantly knew was Pallet glass. And, theoretically, if it were Pallet glass, did Filmore know how to shatter the entire building? Below it and slightly farther was a massive body of water with thin glass bridges. I turned to ask Cupid what it was, but learned that the group was walking ahead of me. The conversation was dizzying, and made complete sense given Cupid's personality.

"I'm actually starving. Do you guys wanna go to—" Cupid started.

"Polly's?!" Hampton said, energetically.

They squealed like girls, and I was immediately snapped back into the gay whirlwind of rich, entitled, damaged twinks. Polly's was a short walk away, a hippie vegan restaurant where I got a kale salad and fries. I managed to scarf down half of my sweet potato fries while the three talked. It was what I expected: boys, drugs, parties, gossip, lingo I was never around to understand. How Tyle, the freshman, got his account banned for spreading misinformation, which made my head shoot up as I thought of the last interaction I had with him.

When we left, an hour later, grotesquely dissatisfied and hangry, Froggy said he was meeting up with a couple tonight, and Hampton said he got a table at Lulu's.

"You don't have a man tonight, Q?" Hampton joked to Cupid.

"No, no, not tonight. I know it's surprising." A pack of girls walked past us, their sugary scent trailing behind as Cupid continued talking.

"You know me, with this bomb pussy," he quipped vulgarly, to the amusement of Hampton and Froggy.

I couldn't believe Cupid would make that kind of joke; just as I felt comfortable and related to Cupid, he distanced himself with the most offensive joke. I was curt on the walk to his apartment to a degree that was standoffish.

I checked my watch and realized that I was meeting Peter in twenty minutes, and told Cupid I had to go.

"Oh, wait, like now?"

"Yeah, I um… I'm meeting a pharmaceutical company."

"Oh! How exciting, just… text me when you're done, I'll get a driver." He kissed me on the cheek and glided away. With me pulling up directions on my phone, I walked toward the building.

Cheshire-Yu Therapeutics was, to my surprise, a stainless steel building that seemed to radiate the sun's heat as I stared at the front. The glass windows revealed a vast lobby, with a single desk in front of a massive image of T cells attacking cancer. I recognized it from my junior year lab, where we were tasked with curing a lab rat of cancer. Half the class failed, and Mark was at the top of the class.

Inside, I approached the desk where Ki, warmly smiling in purple lipstick, greeted me.

"Good afternoon, how may I help you?"

"Hi, I'm meeting with—"

"Me. Thank you, Ki." Dr. Cheshire-Yu stood in a deep purple, almost black, suit. His hair was shorter than the last time, and he continued speaking to a now standing Ki, revealing her in a sleek white dress. "Tell Dr. Frashma that I'll be pushing our meeting out. If need be, buy him lunch, or get him tickets to whatever. Teddy, please."

He motioned to follow him before revealing a bank of about ten elevators. The building looked extremely tall, and when he scanned his card and pressed the forty-second floor, I knew he owned the building.

"What brings you to New York? Oh, and please call me Peter. You're on my schedule, so…we're past that. Plus, my teaching days are over."

"Oh, um… visiting a cousin. He goes to Harlequin."

"Ah… the extrovert academy, my wife and I call it."

"Yes, he's very extroverted, very charming and… definitely commands a room."

"I mean, if you want that, then floors twelve to seventeen are all that, media and press and… chatter boxes. Labs on eighteen to twenty-seven and…" He squinted one eye and looked up, thinking. "Thirty-two to thirty-eight."

"Very impressive," I said, before the elevator opened into his office. Where I thought Dr. Ilt's was impressive, I audibly gasped.

It was the size of the Taupe lecture hall, overlooking New York City, with a glass window that wrapped around. The floor was layered with Pallet glass, looking like deep, almost fairy-tale-like blue water. He had multiple white stone desks, multiple computers peppered around the room that had at least four monitors, and large TV screens. At what I assumed to be his main desk, there was a comfortable white chair that I approached, marveling at the various projects on the screens, maps, papers, and tables. I didn't know if I could read them, but he chuckled with his hands in his pockets.

"I can tell this is the career for you, yes?"

"Without a doubt, yes." He walked to a station in the corner and poured himself tea, offering me a cup, and then walked two steaming cups of green tea to his desk.

"Now, where we were. Oh, yes, you want to talk about…" He sat down, stirring the sugar cube into the glass cup.

"BEV, and what you know," I blurted out, not wanting to string it out any longer. I wanted to make the best use of my time.

Peter inhaled and unbuttoned his suit before sitting. "Well, Mr. Clawik, I found some key biomarkers in my lab, the thirty-eighth floor one to be specific. They found…" He clicked on a tablet and projected to the monitor nearest us, with the entire code that I struggled to comb through, seeming to have cohesive comments, edits, suggestions, and even doodles of animals on it.

"They found that somebody in your lab, Dr. Ilt's lab, made it. We know this from the… biomarkers… here…here… and here." He clicked every time he said this, revealing highlighted Arabic, Braille, and Latin letters that meant nothing to me. "See, every virus has some sort… signature."

"I… um… can you tell… who made it?"

His head twisted to me, and he inhaled through his nostrils. "Are you here to see if you did it, Teddy? Because they already know you did, and not because of me."

"How do they know?"

"Printing logs, video footage. Do I have to show you exactly where it incriminates you?" Peter's tone was stern, and my leverage was now pulverized. I was truly now at his intellectual mercy, and meeting with him to understand how to do damage control, how to understand what information they had, backfired.

"But… I'm the cure to it."

"The cure?" He sipped with a general tone of disbelief.

"Whenever I touch people that have their eyes… colored, it goes away."

"That's not… what? How is that possible? Wait a second." He clicked some letters on his Hexboard, spinning it and stopping it, typing, spinning, stopping, at a lightning speed. With his hand resting on his chin, he looked at the code and then looked at me.

"How did… wait. Do you have your laptop? If you do… can you send me the virus you coded? Do you have it?"

"I…"

This was fully giving all evidence of my crime; this was the smoking gun. Still, in the impressive office, him making time, and the fact that I was suddenly on a first-name basis with him, I decided to send it to him. When he projected the virus on the screen, he clicked a couple of items, running a couple of diagnostics, before a bright red banner appeared at the bottom of the seventy-inch screen. Even though I wasn't keeping up, I could understand the banner almost completely.

"Your biomarkers aren't the same as the BEV patients; this isn't the same virus. Not even close, even with the mutations."

The entire space was silent. The air was still as I looked at him, scanning the code, scrolling, clicking, highlighting, reading.

"What does that mean?"

"You are sure this was the virus you printed, the one you injected into yourself?"

"Yes, absolutely. And, wait, how did you then say it was me? Did they tell you?"

"When I got the virus sample from… that Taupe girl…"

"Moxy."

"Yes, her, Moxy. Odd name, but anyways. I immediately found the code and noticed that it had… these biomarkers are consistent. It's always…" His mind seemed scrambled, and he clicked a box on the side, which said "ORIGIN MARK" and found a series of Greek letters, alongside numbers and Latin letters. "Right here. Dr. Ilt's lab always starts with Beta miu, 45, then some number, always after the viral genetic material. Everything that comes from her lab has that code. Mine is Alpha zeta 29; every pharmaceutical company and major immunotherapy manufacturer has one.

"Well… what about the PharmD students?" Peter was now standing after putting his suit jacket on his chair.

"No, they have three Greek letters and three numbers, because they have manufacturing rights to their pathogens. In your case, BEV always had Beta miu 454. Here, you have Beta miu 453. So, it was made in her lab, and I just stopped there. I didn't have your virus to compare, because I didn't need it."

I squinted at the screen, my eyebrow beginning to twitch.

"And… it's not Dr. Ilt?"

"No," he said, firmly. "And well, since you're the only one working there, I figured that you were the one who made it."

I stood and ran my hands on my face, looking at the tall, almost infinite ceiling. I turned back to Peter Cheshire-Yu, all before he recognized my stress.

"You do… work alone in that lab, correct?"

After I left and finished smoking three cigarettes, I texted Cupid the address where I was. I had walked a bit, almost by Harlequin's campus, and felt a headache coming on. I explained to Peter about Mark, how he worked there too, how I didn't use his viral code biomarker, and how this was, without a doubt, not my virus. I explained how I didn't steal his laptop to make it, and how Mark was the only person I could imagine to produce this. He explained that he never knew about Mark, and Dr. Ilt only implied that I was her only research assistant currently at Taupe. When I brought up Moxy matching my virus, he shrugged and said that my standard name for the virus I designed could be shared by hundreds of viruses. That, and I would learn this if I got into the doctoral program, the advanced name and code is the only way to know if a virus is identical. My last question was about why I was different, why Cupid was different with our genetic code, why we had specific stress triggers. Peter didn't have an answer to that and gestured for me to leave. After waiting about ten minutes, a black car picked me up, one that was ice-cold within, with a driver who also wore gloves steering a shiny, leather wheel.

"Hello, T-Bear! Come on in, your slippers are right there."

Cupid had changed into a bright pink, short-sleeved bathrobe and slippers, pointing to a black pair that he got me. Entering Cupid's apartment felt like entering an amusement park. My eyes were drawn to the long shelf that sat below a jet black television, adorned with crystal vases. My family had ours locked in a cabinet in the dining room, so seeing them sparkle rainbows onto the room made me feel uneasy, as if they would fall and shatter. The rest of the apartment had chic black and white furniture, melted neon candles, and other neon pink accents, such as the pillows, the blankets, and the place mats. Statues of men about half my height, made of what I assumed was marble, decorated the apartment at random. As I stepped in and admired it, its uniqueness, the sweet smell that reminded me of cotton candy, I nearly tripped over something plush. When I looked down, I assumed it was one of Cupid's sweaters or a pair of slippers. Instead, two sets of ice blue eyes stared at me, slowly moving a plush, dark gray tail.

"When did you get a cat?" I asked in confusion, not knowing what to do.

"Last year, around May." Cupid crouched down to pet the puffy cat. "Her name is Burka."

Before the funeral, the last time I saw Cupid was during Easter at the end of April, so I never heard about it since he didn't bring her up.

"You named your cat Thunderstorm?" I said in English, trying to emphasize how dumb it sounded. I slipped into the shoes Cupid bought me, which were extremely soft.

"What? It sounds cute, and she looks like a storm cloud!" Cupid scooped her in his muscular arms like a baby; her purring could be heard at a distance as I paced the apartment in my slippers. We never had pets growing up, and Cupid's family had a dog for a couple of years before it died suddenly. The idea that Cupid had responsibility didn't register with me, but then again, he was actively transforming after his parents died. He beamed a smile at me.

"Do you want to hold her?" he asked, before placing her in my arms.

I had never held a cat before, and this was the only real interaction I had with one. She was extremely light and puffy, and admittedly, I could see the appeal. She stared into my eyes as I stood still, afraid I would drop her. Burka slowly blinked until her eyes were nearly closed, all the while Cupid took countless pictures.

"Oh… she likes you!" Cupid scratched the top of her head with his sharp, black nails, which he must've gotten done when I was away, intensifying her purrs.

He took her back before gently placing her on the couch and leading me to the balcony that overlooked the city, albeit not to the effect of Peter's office. Cupid and I talked about the plans for the weekend, a schedule that didn't seem like a vacation at all. Today was Friday, which meant lines at Lulu's, tomorrow was Spilly's, and Sunday was brunch at Gigi's. It sounded fake to me, like pet names. But, they were actual, real places that held Harlequin's social circles. I pretended to pay attention as I could see, from a distance, the glass arch from Harlequin's campus.

"But… yeah, I want to talk to Lulu today about the pill I made," Cupid said, casually.

"So… that whole pill thing… how did you end up making it?" I asked, curiously.

"You want the truth?" Cupid took a hit of a joint before offering some to me. When I denied, he inhaled and spoke with smoke escaping his mouth, "I told Dr. Pellin that… I had an idea. A time-release sort of pill, one that… well, no, it's boring, science shit." He stopped speaking suddenly, coy and red in the face.

"Cupid…" I assured him. "It's nice to have boring, science shit with somebody else."

He smirked. "You're right. I mean, you have your germs and whatever. But, anyway, I told him that there is a serious problem with… desire. And that, something like this would… revolutionize fertility care in the US. Plus. Dr. Pellin had some code and research from another professor, so it kind of fell into my lap. The base code, at least." I looked at Cupid, and we both knew he was lying about his motives to make the pill.

"Why did you… actually make it? Don't you already have guys… all over you."

"Oh… absolutely all over me, inside me, below me, on top of me. But… I wanted to actually have a say, you know? To actually—"

"Control it," I said, in disbelief. The same desire for control that led me to make my stress virus was shared by Cupid, albeit in a different avenue of our lives.

"And… where did this… expertise… come from?" I asked blankly.

"Well… I always thought that like… drugs were like…" He giggled before resuming his speech, "That drugs were cool."

"Oh, we know," I joked, which was followed by a playful punch to the arm.

He got suspended in high school for dealing drugs, but returned about a week later as if nothing had happened. On his balcony, stories up, we could see thick, dark clouds rolling in slowly toward the city.

"No like… to think that everything in life is… like… chemical. That was always… that fascinated me." Cupid's eyes were now cherry red and squinted, which made me chuckle to myself.

I looked down at my house slippers, mine were woolen, while his were rabbit fur. It was mandated at our grandparents' house that we had house shoes, and I'm glad we carried the tradition overseas. While he was smoking weed, I almost liked him more. Cupid, not being so fast-paced and being calmed down, made him extremely easy to talk to. He wasn't toned down, wasn't muted. Simply relaxed, like somebody had cooled him off and washed away any pressure from him.

"I had… no idea that you were so smart at that," I admitted honestly.

We were both facing the city, and I watched him inhale before turning to me, "Yeah, well… I finally have the space to…actually explore it."

I couldn't exactly tell what he meant, but I let it go in an attempt not to overthink. After everything with Peter, I didn't want any more complications, any more nuance. Any more surprises.

Inside, Cupid said I could nap on the couch, which my tense body seemed to melt into. The lush, ribbed fabric seemed to contort around my body, as the sweet smell of the apartment blended with the lilac fabric softener that we both used. He went to his bedroom, right before grabbing the meowing Burka in his arms.

"My sweet little angel baby that could never do any wrong, I love you to the moon and back, my little angel baby."

After a moment of silence, a single meow caused Cupid to coo affectionately and take her into his room. As he closed the door, I realized that his accent had changed a little bit. He sounded more melodic, softer than usual. I continued to look around, noting the photo of his mother when she was younger, around our age, likely the age that she met my mother. My mother and Cupid's mother were neighbors when they both graduated from college in Slovakia. My mother was trying to study for medical school admission exams, and when Avana's band kept her awake, my mother politely asked her to quiet down. They would tell that story at every family event with a new detail; either the state of Avana's apartment, or what my mother was wearing. Still, it made perfect sense that Cupid's mother annoyed my mother by being too loud, and the rest being history.

I woke up from the nap, refreshed, warm, and with the couch cushions imprinted on my arms. There stood Cupid in a red towel, reminding me of the jealousy I always felt toward his physical physique. My thin, dark brunette hair falling to my receding hairline compared to his bouncy curls. His eyes were the color of traffic signs; mine were the color of moss. Cupid smiled, using another small towel to scrunch his curls.

"Oh, good, you're awake. Morning, princess." Cupid's upper body was built like a swimmer, with minimal chest hair and sculpted muscles.

"What time is dinner?" I yawned, looking at my phone.

No notifications, which was a relief. Nothing from Angel, but that also meant she wasn't in the hospital. Nothing from Dr. Ilt or Mark, which made me even more relieved.

"I called and managed a reservation at Lamb and Butcher in…" Cupid looked at the oven's clock. "Twenty minutes."

"Twenty!? Jesus, Cupid, you should've woken me up!" I rushed into the shower, reminded of my deep fear of being late.

There were four different knobs in the shower, and it wasn't until I turned on the wall jets and the wand that the overhead shower started. Cupid was moving hangers in his bedroom down the hallway, which was decorated with various vintage pornographic models.

"Oh, it's fine, you'll be fine. I'll just call them and lie."

Inside his shower, the products that came in heavy bottles, alongside razors, an empty pink wine glass, and no sign of any bar of soap. I didn't want to have my hair turn red, so I shouted to him in my underwear.

"Cupid!"

"Yeah?" he shouted back from the kitchen.

"What... which shampoo do I use?"

"Oh... coming." I could hear him set down a bowl for Burka and make his way to the bathroom. He studied the bottles from the doorway until pointing to a black one.

"That one. Use that one. It will make your hair bouncy, and smell... fucking amazing."

He was right, I worked the pearl colored liquid into a lather that made the entire bathroom smell like decadent caramel and candy. The body wash, which he instructed to use with the specific blue towel, was also some sort of marshmallow, lemon scent, and admittedly felt nice to indulge myself. I kept smelling my arm after rinsing, and when I stepped out of the shower. I ruffled my hair and studied Cupid's army of products. Cupid was vanity-obsessed; that was clear, but I was beginning to understand why. The different creams on his mantle made his skin smooth, the different shampoos, I'm sure, kept his hair at its best, and the perfumes that I knew would give me a cavity. An arsenal of beauty products to maintain his vanity for Harlequin.

"So… where are we going tonight, after dinner?" I toweled my hair as Cupid put on eyeliner, swearing and grabbing a cotton swab.

"It's a place called Lulu's… it's a line bar right around the main campus. Also, your suit is on the couch."

"Line bar? And, wait, I'm not gonna fit in a suit from you," I said, confused.

"No, it should fit. I saw it, and I thought of you, kind of a… condolences gift." My chest felt bizarre as I walked into the living room, and the freshly pressed suit lay next to the folded blanket. Burka lay in a ball on it, and as I approached it, I heard Cupid get up.

"Do you like… Oh, come on, Burka."

He hoisted her up and shook the suit, tiny hairs falling from it like feathers. There were dark brown shoes and a matching leather belt, a white shirt, and a somewhat lace-looking green tie. The suit was a dark blue and moss green houndstooth, with double lapels that looked expensive. I was never somebody who indulged in fashion, but Cupid handing me the sturdy fabric stunned me.

"Oh my God… this is gorgeous, Cupid."

"Well… your mother did make that coat for my mother, way back when. And she loved it. So this is me… sort of returning the favor."

He waltzed back into his bedroom, as I heard him stomp into his shoes, an annoying habit he had because he never wanted to tie his shoes as a child. I put on the crisp white shirt and moss green tie and buttoned the pearl buttons on the jacket. I knelt to tie my dress shoes, catching myself in the mirror that stood in the hallway. In my father's glasses, with my hair gelled and suit pressed, I stood there. When Cupid stepped out, he wore a suit that looked like a vintage map print. It looked gaudy but chic, only something Cupid could pull off. In sparkling ruby loafers, Cupid breathed out as he saw me in disbelief.

"You look like your dad, oh my God."

And I did, at least in this moment. Old pictures of my father from the military looked like me. I shared a lot of traits with my father: the attention to detail, small handwriting, quietness. Yet, it could easily be seen that I didn't go down a path of finance, but of medicine. That partition made me closer aligned to my mother, in the body of a younger Gregor Clawik.

At dinner, we both got filet mignon, albeit on the different end of the temperature spectrum, with mashed potatoes and garlic asparagus. The restaurant was a somewhat fancy one, with red velvet booths, paintings of European cities, and the light buzz of conversation. There was a singer and pianist by the bar, who sat people in suits, dresses, and wrinkles. The crowd was particularly older, which is what puzzled me. Normally, I would think that Cupid would pick a trendy restaurant. We locked eyes, both mid-chew, when it dawned on me.

"Wait… aren't you vegan?"

"Only in front of Hampton and Tyle." He grabbed the bulbous glass of red wine, raising his eyebrows as he smiled.

"Yeah… they convinced me to do it, but I really can't drop steak like that. They would never come here, which is a plus. They don't eat anything with milk or eggs. Like, can you imagine I stopped eating omelets?"

I couldn't, because his mother made the best omelets I had ever had. She would use the freshest eggs and use some combination of cheese that I'm sure only Cupid knew.

"It was… what was it?" I asked him, point-blank, because I had to know.

He was snapping his fingers and looking up, and I drank my wine. "OH! It was Gruyère, cheddar, some kind of Brie! From the deli down the hill, oh my God. That's what it was. Yeah, those were so good."

The rest of the night, we really started to bond over being Slovak. We talked about his cousins and joked that we shouldn't say too much because his eyes might turn purple.

It was tempting to bring up the entire scenario about Mark and BEV, since it was the right amount of drama that Cupid would crave. Still, the dinner made me forget about the current virus, and it wasn't until the waiter kept filling our waters, asking us about the meal repeatedly, and would spark up conversation that I understood what was happening.

"I think the waiter wants to fuck you." Cupid didn't look at me when he spoke.

"Really? You think?"

"Absolutely. He kept glancing at you and smiling."

I blushed and rolled my eyes. The suit was a glance into Cupid's confident world of delusion, of effortless sex appeal. I was never used to that kind of attention.

"So… how was Indigo? Why did they make you go there?"

"Oh…they wanted Mark and me to… help them with an outbreak. It's really bad there."

"Mark? Mark who?"

"Drykovczynski," I said, trying not to give too much away.

"Never heard of him, is he…?" Cupid added.

"Indigo was horrible. The students hate Russian people, which I didn't know. They seem so… military-like online and everywhere, and it makes sense. It's soul-crushing."

"That… that's horrible."

I could tell Cupid hesitated before speaking, but he spoke earnestly about how bad he felt for the students there. He couldn't imagine, he explained, what it would be like to go there, but had a realization as the waiter cleared the empty dish of mashed potatoes we devoured.

"Wait, just you two went? Mark? Oh, because you work in… oh, that Ilt lady's lab."

"Well… that and we're the finalists for the doctoral cohort, the PharmD spot."

Cupid stopped chewing his steak and looked at me, with some steak juice coming from the corner of his mouth. He swallowed, not breaking eye contact.

"You… got in? Oh my GOD!" Cupid's voice caused multiple people to look over, while I quickly grabbed his arm.

"No, Cupid, no. I'm the finalist; it's between Mark and me."

"Do you want me to…?" His eyes widened as he picked up his phone, like he wanted to do something awful to better my chances, not knowing that I already did something awful.

"No, no, I want this to be on my own. They… well, Dr. Ilt should make a decision during this week…"

"Oh my God, that's… wow. You know, I was thinking of applying to the pharmacy doctor program, too. Albeit with Dr. Pellin's lab."

"Really? That's exciting. I mean, you are… really smart in class. And the fact you made that pill, that's… wow."

"It wasn't that hard, considering BRIAR-M is pretty intuitive. You just… have to know the basic map of the brain, the chemicals and their structures, and that's it."

After dinner, I pressed Cupid about taking me on a tour of campus. Past the metal gothic gates stood a green jester statue, which Cupid said was malachite, in a square body of water the size of a large swimming pool. Around the water, and the source of the floral smell that hit my nose when we stepped on campus, were daffodils, yellow ones. There must have been hundreds of them making the air smell floral and slightly bitter, but my gaze went upward. Finally, the arch I had been seeing was in front of me. There were two buildings that were also clear, standing tall and connected to each other at the top. Lights within made it appear slightly golden, like the color of champagne. In the shape of an upside-down U, the building gleamed as students could be seen sitting at clear tables, a group of students huddled around a clear desk about two hundred feet up.

"That's Glacier. Our library. People don't go there to study; they only show families. Only REAL die-hard students go there. I mean, I haven't been inside since sophomore year."

I couldn't keep my eyes off the structure. The more I looked, the more I fell in love. It sparkled intoxicatingly; my eyes couldn't ignore it. It had a long walkway that connected the two towers around the front and back. I could see people strolling on the top and taking pictures of the skyline.

"Where do you do your homework?" I asked, staring at the group of friends on the glass bridge.

"My apartment, or I hire somebody who… probably is in there." He chuckled with stained teeth, clearly intoxicated from dinner's wine.

The right of the jester fountain was the real estate building and marketing building, with a pathway separating the schools and connecting to the Glacier. There was the neon graphic design building, and the media building, which was a tall, black cylinder building. Cupid explained there were no dorms directly on campus, aside from two towers for freshmen, but bragged that the main green was a sight. About the size of two tennis courts was another body of water, with thin, glass bridges that connected over it. As if somebody shot arrows across the water, their paths were crystal bridges. Cupid and I turned right and walked to the hill that overlooked both parts of campus, the Glacier reflecting on the water and the daffodils moving slightly in the breeze.

"Holy shit… this is gorgeous," I said, in awe. It was a complete contrast to Indigo and the environmental horrors that were on that campus.

"Right? I fucking love it." Cupid pulled out a blue box of cigarettes, accompanied by a white lighter. Cupid passed me the cigarette. The last time we smoked together, it was on the rooftop bar in Slovakia.

"You know… today is…." Cupid turned to me, his arms spread over the back of the bench.

"Yeah."

There was a pause, and then I spoke after dragging on the cigarette.

"I know."

It had been one month since the bombing. The air between us shifted, and Cupid broke the silence in a sincere tone.

"It's kinda crazy to think… that… the reason that we're here… isn't here, y'know? That like… they won't see us graduate, or all the money they made… they don't see that."

"Yeah… it's um…"

I felt myself crying, and then Cupid's arms around me, being engulfed in a smell that was cinnamon and raspberry. That my mother and father wouldn't see how smart I'd become, how Cupid's parents wouldn't see him thrive, and they both wouldn't see how both of their kids were building a life for themselves at the world's best universities. How their son was a finalist to be a doctor at a school that was beyond reach to get into. And how Cupid was working in a lab and being light years ahead of people in the class, all while studying at Harlequin. It was a sweet moment, until Cupid received a text from Hampton and jolted back into his usual, dopamine-craving self.

In the taxi, Cupid explained how Lulu's Line Bar worked. Basically, the Pallets turned a blind eye to about ten bars around the campus that had old, or outdated, pill manufacturing machines from Taupe. They were machines that were coded for specific drug recipes, meaning they have been the same for over twenty years. We would go to the farthest one, since it was the most exclusive. They had the same drug recipes since the first one opened, so it was trusted and safe. I was extremely skeptical and told Cupid that I didn't want to go, nor partake. Cupid insisted that because I wanted to experience Harlequin authentically, a line bar was a must. Maybe the intense party culture was the reason there weren't cases, and created an environment that was stress-free.

On the way to the line bar, Cupid told me how much money he'd been spending recently. On haircare, crystal decor, clothing, booze, new appliances, skin care, sex toys, drugs. It baffled me, even a month later, how much money we each got. His wallet was all 100 and 50-dollar bills, and he struggled to close the zipper on it. We laughed at his student ID, which he looked fetal in. After showing him mine and laughing about it, we left the car after Cupid gave the man a hundred dollars for a drive that was less than a mile. Lulu's Line Bar glowed in a neon orange sign, and I could hear cackling inside. Cupid explained to me that this was an exclusive one, and only upperclassmen with connections could get in. I didn't want to ask how Cupid had connections, but it was slightly intriguing to watch.

"So, Hampton is inside waiting. We'll go to the bar…"

"I'm not getting anything," I told Cupid, firmly in Slovak.

A long car unloaded more eccentric students, all in some variation of a fur coat, stumbled into the line. It was about fifty people at this point, and Cupid was becoming irritated with my boundary.

"Yes, Virgin Mary, I heard you. Anyways, we have our table. We'll go to the bar…"

"But I'm not—"

"Jesus, Teddy! I know! You're not gonna get anything, fuck! Just… pretend! Sneeze, drop your platter, I don't care!" Cupid was trying to remain silent, but was drawing attention from people who didn't understand Slovak.

"No! I am not getting anything at all! I don't understand how this is even legal, don't the Pallets care?"

"Oh God no, they don't give a shit. I've heard Hawley's son comes here sometimes and gets a booth in the back. But, listen…" Cupid sighed dramatically before lecturing me, "Just go to the bar, Lulu is working tonight. Order a line, it can be a sober one, and bring it to the table."

"Excuse me?" A student behind us tapped me on the shoulder, interrupting us. "Are you guys like... what language is that?" The guy with way too many necklaces on his neck giggled and tossed his white hair.

"It's Slovak," Cupid stated coldly, descending one of the steps.

"Oh shit, no way! With all that... brutal shit going on, that's crazy. Well... it sounds like... super fucking cool. Can I get a recording of you talking? I know it's on the spot, but..." The person had green gems on all his teeth, as well as one piece of his black hair matching Cupid's eyes.

"Oh, no, we were..." I tried to avoid it, but Cupid eagerly replied, pushing my back against the railing.

"Sure, we can," Cupid interrupted. In Slovak, Cupid and I talked with the camera flash on. We talked about the weather, what we were wearing, with Cupid guiding most of the conversation. It was an extremely forced conversation, one out of a textbook. The person recording stopped and seemed amazed.

"This is going to be perfect for the Jester. We've wanted to do something about the crisis, but... we didn't know you were from there!"

Cupid and the guy, whose name was Isiah, spoke English at an extremely fast pace. It was like watching reality television at double speed, with a vague veil of intellect that could be felt every so often. He studied media and was taking a class with Francesca Briar next semester in order to cover mental health medication news. At the door, Cupid kissed one girl on the cheek before having the door opened for us.

"Those media idiots cut the line," he muttered in Slovak, as I stepped into the purple-lit jungle that reeked of synthetic bubble gum.

Hampton stood at the front of the spacious jungle of plastic leaves, in a cheetah print suit. There were leopard print couches that sat students in elegant attire. To my shock, I watched a girl in a blue gown snort a line of some powder from a glowing yellow acrylic tray. I became fixated on her, expecting her to faint or her nose to bleed. I had never seen somebody snort anything aside from movies, and watching it happen in real life terrified me. My fixation was interrupted by Hampton, who hugged hard and pressed his rings into my back.

"TA Cousin's in town to party! Hello, honey bee!" Hampton was clammy and smelled like a spicy cologne. I pulled away from the suit, which turned out to be silk.

"Hi Hampton. It's great to see you again. How are... things?" I asked awkwardly. I had very little social tact, especially after watching the girl in blue. Next to her, I watched another girl dump powder from her fingernail into her eye, shaking her head quickly with her mouth wide open.

"Things are peachy keen! Class is fine, and practices have been canceled for some time, that... virus thing, whatever. But you should be in the lab making my vaccine, slacker! I have to get back on the field!" He playfully punched my arm, and I had no words to respond.

Is that how they saw Taupe students? Just lab rats to work for them? To make sure they are healthy? Before I could respond, Cupid dragged me to the bar and passed cohorts of people around low tables. Some lounging, some holding neon trays to noses. I was extremely overwhelmed until I saw the bartender.

"Hello, baby, whatcha want?" A drag queen in a tall, blonde wig blinked at me. Her lips were drawn on a red circle, and she stood at my height in a glittering gold bodysuit.

"Oh... uh... I..." I stammered, awkwardly scanning the menu.

"Get him a sober line, Lulu," Cupid added, which led Lulu to clack her long nails onto a purple tray, dump a white powder, and pop a glass straw into its designated compartment.

I blinked at her sharp nails, not knowing what to do as she held the tray in front of me.

"My arms hurt, twink. Take the tray," she asserted, and asked Cupid for his order.

"Yeah… so… I'll take a… four of Poppy, a ten of Turbo, and… oh! Get me a six of Pillowcase."

"You got it."

I watched Lulu scoop three powders with a small spoon on the tray behind the glass. One glowed under the neon light, a chemical green powder pushed into a line with her nail. I could only imagine what that did in his body, and I didn't want to think about it. There was an extremely low ceiling that made the space seem more intimate, but suffocated me. The smell was slightly tangy and chemical, slightly reminding me of Indigo's putrid smell, but the wafts of random perfumes subdued that. I stared at my tray, a thin white line that was exactly at the six-inch mark of the engraved ruler.

"What is this?" I asked Cupid over the jazz music that started playing.

"It's a B vitamin. You're not gonna get high, I promise."

"I said I didn't…"

"Listen… I'll do it for you, okay? I get it, but… it's how it is here. Go to the bathroom or something, and I'll do it. I wanted… to make sure you felt included. And, if you want booze, there's a liquor bar in the back."

I smiled at the attempt to make me feel included. Maybe grief softened Cupid a little, or maybe he was like that all along. We walked to the table, and I dropped off the tray. I told Hampton and him that I had to use the bathroom, and they told me it was down the hall. After weaving past groups of laughing patrons, there was a line, full of people in gowns, gaudy necklaces, animal print suits, and skinny fit clothing. The girl in front of me was by herself, wearing a dress that had extreme cleavage. It was hard to ignore that everybody at Harlequin was fit. Physical appearance was extremely coveted, and I washed my hands next to a guy with massive, tattooed arms.

"Move! I have to piss, morons!" Tyle exclaimed, slamming into the door and nearly cracking my nose as I stood by the sink. It took him a second to register, and when his eyes focused on me, his demeanor changed.

"Oh… it's this one. What the fuck are you doing here?" Tyle's suit was a black and white animal print of some sort, partially glowing under the lighting of the bathroom.

"I'm um… visiting a cousin." I dried my hands with thick tissue, dispensed from a zebra's butt.

"Your cousin? Who is it, Jack Frolly?" I never heard that name before, but people around me laughed as they put mascara on in the mirror. Tyle was checking his phone as he used the urinal, while the guy at the next urinal was doing a line of his own on the top of the urinal.

"No, bitch, he means me." I could smell Cupid before I turned around, with the air becoming fruity as horror flickered on Tyle's face, before resolving to his normal arrogance.

"Oh… the accents. That makes sense." Tyle shrugged, and I watched Cupid's face turn into something evil. He looked like his father now, with wrinkles appearing on his smooth forehead. I urged Cupid to leave, but something changed in the past ten minutes. Tyle zipped his pants and sized Cupid up.

"I like that suit on you, Cue. Not something I would wear, but…"

"Look who's talking, with that cheap suit and color job." Cupid plucked at Tyle's new cyan hair, but he was stumbling over his accented words. Tyle taunted his accent by parroting back what he said. I knew that Cupid hated his accent more than anything, and being at a school like Harlequin meant that it was fair game to be mocked.

"Cupid, you're high. Let's go…" I tugged his blazer, urgent to leave the hostile situation.

"Yeah, listen to whatever… Russian or whatever bullshit your cousin is saying," Tyle added, splashing his hands with water. Cupid took a second, shaking his head.

"We're not going to talk about your canceled segment?"

I could immediately tell this changed the mood of the conversation, and people started to stare as Cupid continued to belittle the first year.

"Ty Ty, your eyes look a little inky…! You kind of look like a glassblower! Oh, wait, no. You're not blowing glass… we all know who you are blowing," Cupid taunted cruelly.

I could see Tyle's face become clammy as laughter bounced off the walls, and I swore that Tyle's eyes became slightly yellow, flickering fluorescently very briefly. The fact that Harlequin students knew about the virus and the inky colored eyes was frightening, but even worse was that they started to bully people for it. The outbreak hadn't even started three weeks ago, which proved how fast information spread at a place like Harlequin. It dawned on me that Indigo's stress was a quota, Taupe's main stress must have been grades, and Harlequin's main stressors must have been other people and their opinions. Cupid rolled his eyes again, winking and smiling at me like nothing happened.

There was a moment of silence, both of them staring at each other, breathing heavily, before Tyle's sclera sparkled brightly again, back to normal. I expected Tyle to slam Cupid into the paper towel dispenser, and for Cupid to drive his nails into Tyle's eye sockets. I tugged on Cupid one more time anxiously, before locking eyes with me. His eyes were glassy, like when he was smoking on the porch. When he turned back to Tyle, Cupid inhaled as the tension was at its peak. I thought Cupid would throw the first punch, right at Tyle's throat.

But, they both laughed poshly, like everything they just said was a joke. People around them went back to their normal business, putting on lipstick or taking pictures in the long bathroom mirror.

Tyle and Cupid hugged, with the little freshman staring at my cousin as he spoke, "Oh… you bitch, love you Cupid. You are always so… funny to me. My eyes are good though, yeah?"

"Oh yeah, you're fine. I'll see you on the couch? I'm by the front."

"Yes! Shirley, Kelly, and I have a table in the back, but… I'll bring us some lines… okay?"

They kissed on the cheek, and Cupid motioned me to go, as I began to process the whiplash that just happened. When I got back to the table, Hampton was doing a line while I asked Cupid to explain what occurred with Tyle.

"Oh, that? Nobody really hates anybody here… I mean, publicly. Tyle is fine, he's just… annoying. But, we save all the actual… resentment, that's a good word for it, for online. The media professors are bullies enough, and they are the ones we hate." I adjusted myself on the faux leather couch, trying to make sense of it all.

"I'm confused. So, you like Tyle? He's your friend?" I watched a waitress bring the table next to us a round of colorful cocktails, which immediately made me want one to handle the emotional pressure I was processing. I could never have that banter with Moxy or Mark without some sort of repercussion. The level of verbal venom was extremely out of place at Taupe and could lead to expulsion.

"I mean, no. I don't like him at all, but he won't know that. But, once again, did he say something online? No. Did he mouth off to a professor or a signing agent? Not that I know of. So… banter like that… it's expected." Cupid said cooly, with Hampton nodding as if he were profound. To me, it felt deeply flawed.

"Teddy… everybody here is fake, that's why we're all happy." Cupid pressed his nose and snorted the neon orange line.

A cocktail waitress brought us a bottle of champagne, courtesy of Tyle. The bottle had streaks of neon green that glowed under the ceiling light, since Pallet glass symbolically had a distinct neon green ingredient. As I handled the bottle, Cupid's state changed, from irritating and persistent to calm.

"Plus… I should have told Tyle to get a razor and make his forearm a bar code!" Cupid said in English, which amused a cackling Hampton.

A boy walked by Hampton, before grazing his open shirt. Hampton's head turned and followed the guy, who winked at him. I was startled by how cruel Cupid was, and how Hampton fed into it.

"God… do us the favor, please!" Hampton chuckled as he played with his nose before changing the subject after it went silent.

"Teddy… this is awesome. I am so glad you're here." He hugged my side as I twisted the bottle open, sending the cork into the leaf-covered ceiling. It nearly missed one of the hanging UV lanterns, which dangled throughout the space.

"Mm! Teddy was telling me that he went to Indigo and…" Cupid said.

"Oh my God, I heard they work them like dogs. And, they're assholes! And too, somebody told me once that they castrated them…" Hampton chimed in, while I drank silently.

"They chop their dick off?!" Cupid then described various mutilations in extreme detail.

"Isn't that horrible! Could you imagine!" Hampton and Cupid laughed cynically, and it was entertaining to watch them banter.

It was maddening to see how little they knew about Indigo, and if they didn't go to Taupe, I could only imagine what they would say about us. The two named people they would want to be castrated, adding extremely explicit details on what they heard about their sex lives. Hearing the way they talked about guys was unsettling. Cupid made comments about somebody's body count, while Hampton made comments about their weight and belly. I was borderline nauseous thinking about how objectifying, how ruthless they were, and silently sipped my champagne. I could only imagine what they said about me, which unsettled me more when Hampton put me in the hot seat.

"And what about you? Are you with... anybody?" his words were slurred, his pupils dilated extremely.

"No. I'm single, school kind of..."

"Oh, blah blah, we all have school, we all have things to do! You just have to get laid!" Cupid shook me violently, which made me uneasy.

I thought about Mark, but there was absolutely no way I would tell them about how I slept with the other PharmD contender, one that I destroyed. Let alone my academic rival. It would invite questions about what happened that I didn't trust Hampton with, let alone Cupid. In the middle of their banter, Lulu rang some sort of bell that summoned drag queens dressed like maids to dance on the bar.

"We have to go to Spilly's tomorrow!" Cupid stood up with his eyes focused on Hampton.

"Yes! Oh my God!" Hampton agreed, grabbing his shoulders.

Whatever Spilly's was, I could only imagine that other loud, bright, flashy, overwhelming nightclub it was. When Hampton took off his blazer, his arm muscles caught my attention. When he caught me staring at them, he sat down right next to me, putting his arm around me. Luckily, I was interrupted by a drag waitress handing us more champagne, which Hampton asked for directly on his tongue. It wasn't long before I ended up fairly drunk, as more and more flutes were in my hand. I wanted to ask Hampton so many questions, like where it came from. Yet, I was being fed drinks at an alarming rate. I took selfies with Hampton, and I talked to people at the liquor bar in the back. At one point, I even went in for one of the Pallet glass platters with the lines on it. Cupid pulled me by the shirt to stop me and told me that I had drunk enough. I could see why people at Harlequin were so wild, because I have not felt this stress-free since before Taupe. It reminded me of the time I spent with Mark at Indigo, and I suddenly felt the urge to call him. I wanted him, and I didn't care if Dr. Ilt wanted to keep us separated. I don't care about the doctorate program or Peter Cheshire-Yu. I wanted him, I was craving him. The last thing I remembered was staring up at the Glacier in Cupid's arms, the stars above us twinkling and spinning.

Chapter Ten

The next morning, I rubbed my eyes and felt the throbbing headache, the worst headache I had ever had. I was sandwiched between two heavy pillows, and lying on my side in the clothes from last night. My shirt smelled awful, and I hoisted myself up at the singing I heard. Cupid stood in his boxers and a sweatshirt, singing a Slovak pop song that I knew from childhood. His voice was extremely well-balanced, which made sense given his mother's former singing career. I fluttered my eyes while I watched him at the stove, with Burka resting on his arms as he cooked.

"So then, you fluff this a little bit, and then add your pepper…" he explained to the cat, which looked like a baby in his arms.

At one point, he plucked a piece of egg from the pan, blew on it, and fed it to her. Watching Cupid be paternal was something I never expected to witness, but I was happy I did. My loud yawn led him to turn around, beaming a smile.

"It's the party animal! Do you sleep well?" He dropped Burka, who darted right at me. Her breath smelled like egg as she sat right in front of my face. My body felt weak and dehydrated, and I haven't been this hungover since my Taupe send-off party in Slovakia.

"I slept…okay. Jesus, what happened last night? I remember the huge… green, and that's it."

"Well. You threw up on that green, but I held your hair, don't worry. Then I carried you in here, plopped you on the bed, and made sure you didn't throw up. And that was that."

Breakfast was identical to what his mother would cook, except for the scrambled eggs. She would make an omelet, but Cupid knew better than to try to emulate it. On my iridescent plate was bacon, scrambled eggs, rye bread, coffee, and juice. When I asked him if he made pagach to celebrate my arrival, I got a playful punch to the arm.

"Hell no. I'm not ruining my kitchen for that shit. All the flour, God no. I'll leave that behind in Slovakia." Cupid sipped his coffee, wiping his lips on the bright green Harlequin sweatshirt with cigarette burns on the sleeves. "Anyways, Hampton said you had a lot of fun, and invited us to Spilly's tonight."

"I'll see…" I was hesitant, since going to a bar where people snorted lines of drugs did not seem like my scene. My response was quickly rejected by Cupid.

"No, no. Wrong answer. No. We are there. Hydrate, shower, I have some pills to…"

"I got it, okay, okay."

After showering and popping two pain relievers, we did some shopping. It was dizzying to see how Cupid spent money and what he was buying. Thrown over his shoulder was a grotesque amount of tight pants, neon shirts, bedazzled jackets, and other garments, all in different colors and fabrics. This was a designer store, too, and we were starting to get stared at by people whose idea of luxury was a belt. I noticed it, and then Cupid noticed me.

"Oh… too much?" He smiled at me, speaking English.

At the checkout, it was another girl Cupid knew, albeit not from Harlequin. She was ordinary-looking, plain in the same designer she was selling. Cupid insisted I lump our purchases together, and when she revealed the total, I swallowed dryly. I could never imagine spending that on clothing. Around us, I noticed one person snapping their neck with a single short-sleeved shirt in their arms. When Cupid carried out four bags, my face reddened as we walked back to his apartment.

Crossing the street, a car slammed on its brakes as Cupid crossed in front of them. It was way too close for my comfort, and Cupid ended up spitting ruthless things at them with his finger up. Growing up, Cupid was always lively and silly, never mean or nasty. He would joke about our grandfather's hair being frizzy or talk about video games he wanted to play. He sat politely and had manners, which oddly contrasted with his parents' bickering at the table. And now, he began to tell me about random people and how much he didn't like them. I nodded, observing the shift from the silly cousin to the cruel one.

The rest of the day, we spent at Cupid's place with Hampton as I focused on the jacket embroidery. After I bought a single designer jacket, I decided I wanted to add snow on the trees on the back. From the droplet of conversation I actually registered, I realized that Hampton barely had a personality and kept chirping about the guy he's been talking to. I was focused on creating the snow on the trees, intently focusing on the fabric near my face. Hampton sat in gray sweatpants and a white tank top, crisscrossed, intently listening to me when I would say a handful of words.

"So… like… what is Taupe like? I mean, I have a glimmer of it as your student, but…"

"You should fail him!" Cupid shouted over a blender. American pop music was playing on the TV, with a peach-scented candle lit on the dinner table.

"Oh shut up! That smoothie isn't going to help with that back acne!" Hampton snapped back. I was grateful I didn't have to be at Harlequin, given how caddy it was. Plus, Angel and I were too tired with work to even be remotely mean to each other. Hampton turned to me again and repeated the question as he sipped his white wine.

"Oh… it's fine. Kinda… awful, actually," I answered shyly, and pulled the needle through the fabric of my hoodie.

Burka hopped on my lap, circling before sitting on my lap, staring at me. She seemed to be glaring at Hampton.

"What? Really? I'm sorry…" Hampton put his hand on my shoulder, and I darted my eyes at Cupid. He was in the kitchen, chopping strawberries for his smoothie.

"It's fine… honestly, I just do my work and keep to myself," I continued.

"You don't have friends? That's hard to believe…" Hampton cooed.

I laughed, and Hampton blinked at me. We talked about my classes and Slovakia. I asked him about his heritage, and he claimed he was loosely Greek on his dad's side.

"I mean… I know Cupid doesn't talk much about Slovakia," continued Hampton.

"What?" I said, shocked.

Being Slovak was extremely difficult for us to hide, given how we talked. And since Cupid tokenized everything, I was slightly confused.

"Yeah… he says it's homophobic."

"Which it is," Cupid called from the kitchen, talking over the loud blender.

"Oh… I never had a problem…" I stated.

"That's because you don't dress like a hooker. And you don't… want to dress like this." Cupid gestured to the hot pink outfit he had just purchased.

We all smirked and laughed, but it was true. When I would go to Slovakia and see Cupid, it was as if he were a different person. He never wore tight clothing, never wore anything feminine. Even on the private plane ride, he was rubbing acetone over his fingers. The truth was, Cupid didn't dress like this over there, and I've never seen him in bright colors when we were home.

"I never really… thought of it…"

I hadn't, frankly.

My family was the same way, but I was never the type, even in America, to be feminine. The most homophobic encounter I experienced in Slovakia was dirty stares from old women when I wore my purple Converse one April, and after that, I decided to never wear them. But then again, whenever I was asked about a girlfriend, I said no; whenever people had set me up with women, I said that Taupe was too hard to have a relationship, especially one across the world. By the time I came out, my mother and father sat me at the dinner table, and advised me not to share it.

"We... we love you. And..."

"And I had a gay neighbor in school, and I was fine with it. He helped me with things around my place and made the best cake. So... but... I don't want you to be hurt." My mother sipped her coffee the morning after I told them in their bedroom. They shrugged.

It made sense, and I wasn't hurt by it. I wasn't the type to be outwardly gay, which made life easier.

"But..." My father wagged his finger. "This... isn't an excuse to... slack off."

"Exactly... don't let this... or other people... or... boys... distract you from work, okay?" my mother added, while I nodded.

It felt like a media prep call, a professional debriefing. I walked away, slightly more anxious. Not because my parents were homophobic per se, but because now they could use something against me if I was falling behind. I remember worrying that boys would be the next distraction. Cupid, on the other hand, didn't need to come out, since his personality and mannerisms made it relatively obvious from a young age. I had stuck to the promise I made myself, that boys would never come before work. Aside from that, there weren't really great options at Taupe. All except Mark, who I hadn't heard from and didn't want to bring up. When Hampton left around four, we started to wash the three smoothie cups.

"Hampton definitely wants to fuck you," Cupid said in Slovak, without turning to me.

"Oh... really?"

"Absolutely. He and I are similar in that it's clear as day that we want somebody. He wants you."

"But... I can't sleep with your friend... that's fucked up."

"Eh… it's fine. If you wanted to, of course. If not, I can tell him you're not into him. Hampton has a habit of sleeping with my friends and screwing me over. So, if you want to… go for it." The kitchen went silent, with the only sound being the running water.

"I'm sorry, Cupid. He's my student, so I can't anyway. What did he—"

"Oh, yeah, don't. Hampton would leverage that shit and get you fired."

I quickly became worried about Hampton, what strings he could pull with Dr. Ilt. Cupid looked at me, and smiled how I do when it's awkward, without teeth. He shook his head. "Yeah… Hampton has a habit of fucking guys that either I'm into or are friends with me. The hardest thing is…" He turned off the water, and I watched him with a cup in my hand. "He makes a mess out of everything, every relationship. I can't even see any guys anymore… and I haven't even told him about Reagan yet. The guy from the Taupe party."

"So… why do you keep up with him? Why do you… keep him around?"

"What option do I have? Every gay guy either wants to fuck me, can't hold a conversation, or has some sort of drama with Hammy."

"Right… so being friends with him… is kinda weighing you down, right?

"I guess…" He sat at the table, inhaling a hot pink vape. "I mean… I think I'm just… afraid of him. The shit storm he caused… the rumors. So, I think I keep him close because like… if I kick him to the curb, it's kinda over for me, socially. He's all I have in New York."

Hampton, and a flamboyance of gay people marked the beginning of the pregame about five hours later. There was Froggy, Phoenix, Nate, and Pony, among others, who seemingly blended into each other. The person that I spoke with the most was Phoenix, since he was in the least eccentric outfit in muted, earth tones, and studied interior design. Many of his friends called him boring, but he shrugged and said he still got interviews with interior designers across the world. I left that conversation to find Cupid in his room, wearing his bright pink robe and putting on red eyeshadow that made his eyes pop. His room was picturesque and messy at the same time. White painted walls with the same aesthetic as his living room. He had a neon purple outline of the New York skyline, and a pink rendition of the Slovak flag. His desk had a pink monitor, a pink rubber ducky, and a white keyboard with pink glowing letters. His backpack was designer, some sort of leather with red hearts embroidered on with his initials at the top. I was scanning the room while the sound of pushing hangers and clothes tossing was behind me. It was a sight to see how much character he had. The makeup in a clear bin, the coordinated pink colored office supplies, and pens. It was refreshing to see him with such a brand, such a sense of cohesive style. And then I saw it, and it truly shocked me.

It was a photo of Cupid and his parents at his boarding school graduation. He was holding blue and white balloons, his father a cigar. The three of them looked so happy, all seamlessly coordinated in navy blue. His mother was in a flowing gown, with her colored blond locks. His father, Stefan, was a short and stout man with a rounder face who would greet me with only a handshake. The one trait that was distinguished on Cupid's face was his father's eyebrows; intense and expressive, but they added to Cupid's overall sharp geometry. His father was a welder at an ammunition factory near the hospital. Nobody really had a problem with him unless his patience was tested, resulting in awkward silence and quick words among the adults. But it was nice to see him smiling with his educated, Pallet School-bound son. Now, his son was eyeing me judgmentally as I stood on his lush, pink carpet.

"Are you... wearing that...?"

"Yeah… I have nothing else. Is it okay?" I thought my suit pants and a regular button-up were fine, but Cupid clearly disagreed.

He scoffed at the question and threw clothing at me like a dog. After being practically forced to change, I was wearing a black crop top, feeling ridiculously exposed and vulnerable. You could see my underwear band and hair that went down to my crotch, which Cupid enthusiastically stated was very fashionable. I was in a pair of yellow cargo pants, with the same boots that I wore. When revealing a jewelry box the size of a nightstand drawer, I chose a barbed wire necklace and a matching bracelet. I checked myself out in his mirror, which was decorated with stickers from businesses around the city. I looked nothing like me, I felt nothing like me. I slumped into his desk chair as he debated what clothes to wear with the blue pants he had on, scrolling mindlessly on the Pallet Portal.

"Oh… before I forget." He stepped over a red jockstrap that was on the floor and dropped a small pink pill in my hand. "In case… you know… you wanna hook up with somebody."

He winked at me, and I marveled at it. It looked like rose quartz, only the size of an aspirin pill my grandparents used to give me.

"Is this… limerzine?" I didn't look at him, but watched the small pill roll around my palm.

"Yup. Dr. Pellin already said the Pallets are interested in adding it to their pharmacy portfolio, isn't that cool?" He smiled, whereas I felt dread.

I knew that I didn't know everything, and that they were finding ways to trap Cupid. They found a way to get Cupid enticed with attention and praise, involved in their awful family business. The difference with me was that I saw through it after the conversation with Filmore; the money, the fame. It was about control, which was what I pondered as we walked to the party in a loud, cackling pack of gays.

It was called Spilly's, the so-called gay party house at Harlequin. Shockingly close to the main campus, the house could be heard as soon as we crossed the campus gates. I didn't really know there would be a beach theme, but when I saw boys in bikinis and shirtless guys in swim trunks, I got the sense that we were out of place.

The party smelled like alcohol, room spray, weed, perfume, and when I looked down at my hands, I already had sort of red glitter on them from rubbing up against somebody. It was moderately crowded, with most people being in the blue-lit basement. No flashing lights, only blue, overhead lighting. It was about 90 percent muscular gay men, all around my age. There were people in the corner talking, people making out, people dancing on each other, people just standing there, people dancing with each other. There was jewelry, eye makeup, mini skirts, half of the people were in sunglasses, fruit flavored vape juice, white rum spilled on my pants, pill bags, and condoms on the floor. The four of us stationed ourselves in the center of the dancefloor, bobbing to the music that seemed to change every thirty seconds. I realized I had to pee, which Cupid rolled his eyes at. He didn't want to move, neither did the other two, and I trekked the way upstairs with Cupid behind me, complaining. I locked eyes with a couple of people and smiled at their non-physical advances. I even got complimented on my pants, which felt like a costume at this point. As Cupid said goodbye to me, somebody called for him. He exclaimed and hugged him before kissing him on the lips.

"Teddy! It's Reagan, remember?"

He was the guy Cupid was flirting with weeks ago at the Pallet Ball celebration. He wore a blue mesh tank top and glistened with glittered body oil. I turned away from them and entered the bathroom. Fiber pills, a random frog statue, and a naked woman painting were things that caught my eye as I peed, as well as a bathtub full of ice and glass liquor bottles. It was another reminder of how Pallet glass was everywhere, even in trashy party bathrooms. I didn't want to think about why the room was noticeably warmer than outside, but I flushed and proceeded to walk to Cupid with his arm slung around Reagan.

"Teddy! Teddy! He's..." Cupid hiccuped and continued to attempt talking.

That was when his face changed, his cheeks puffed, and I knew immediately what was happening. I barged into the bathroom with a girl on the toilet, squealing as she left with Cupid throwing up in the sink. Reagan turned to me with concern as I rubbed Cupid's back, much like he probably did to me twenty-four hours ago.

"Relax. He's fine." I told Raegan. Cupid stopped after three rounds and sat on the ground. I looked around for a cup for water, but couldn't find anything.

"Can you just watch him?" Reagan nodded, and I swiftly went downstairs.

The number of people increased dramatically, and it took me five minutes to get to the kitchen cabinet with loose hinges. I found a chipped mug in the kitchen after weaving between people, but put it down once I saw there was a torn case of plastic water bottles underneath a beer pong table. I grabbed three bottles and headed upstairs again.

When I got into the bathroom, Reagan and Cupid were gone. I whipped my head around, starting to panic since I barely knew Reagan, and Cupid was not in a proper state of mind right now to be left with a stranger. I darted around the house, between the various friend groups, the people who forgot deodorant, crunching on plastic cups as I sped through the entire house that seemed to have never-ending living rooms. I pulled out my phone to text Cupid, standing in the atrium of the house with people moving all around me, bumping into me, and one girl spilling her cup on my shoes. With the door completely open, I could see Reagan's back in his blue shirt sparkle while he was outside talking to somebody, with no Cupid next to him. As I went to walk outside to ask him, a muscular shoulder abruptly pushed me aside, with a bottle in his hand.

"Move," Cupid ordered, in English.

With Cupid swigging from the bottle and joining him, I saw who Reagan was now arguing with.

It was Mark.

"What the fuck?" I said under my breath.

Mark was wearing a hoodie, jeans, boots, and a baseball hat. He looked dramatically out of place and held some sort of cube in his hand. As I approached, I saw Cupid take a swig of the bottle while he twisted his head at Mark. Students circled around the heated argument, and it seemed that it was time for a show. One that I did not want to be a part of.

"Oh! Look who the FUCK it is! Little mister victim, little mister stress! Hey buddy!" Mark's head turned as he darted right at me, putting his arm around me so vigorously that it hurt.

"This right here… this is my best friend." Mark wasn't drunk, not that I could tell, but his tone was bitter.

"What are you doing…"

"Well, Teddy…" He patted my shoulder and looked at me, as I noticed a crowd starting to form. "I got news today…well, let me rewind. You called me yesterday! Should I… you know what, let's…"

Mark revealed the cube speaker and played a voicemail from me. It was definitely on the walk back from Lulu's, and I sounded extremely drunk. I was mixing Slovak and English, but I was telling him, in explicit detail, why I wanted him in bed with me. I have never felt more embarrassed or ashamed.

"So, that was my gift this morning. You know what was even… FUCKING better? Getting expelled!" he barked at me through closed teeth, which I recoiled from, then he grabbed my jacket with enough force to make me wince, until he grabbed my throat and pushed me against Spilly's.

"Absolutely not…" Cupid held the bottle in his thighs and took off his earrings.

"I swear to… fucking God. You… took that… from me, Little Miss Dr. Ilt's pet. Oh my god, I wanted you out of there so badly. She fucking LOVES you, couldn't get enough of you. I tried everything to stress you out. I… started this thing, I made you believe I liked you…. I just want to watch you get sick and watch your eyes, darken one… last… time. And, you made it so easy by leaving your blood in the machine."

With his other hand, he pressed his phone and a Russian newscast. As I closed my eyes, trying to calm myself, I tried to ground myself. I told myself it wasn't real, that the hands around me weren't real, that Russians weren't here. I felt my body temperature rise, my eyes become feverish, and I looked at Mark's smiling face. Cupid stood behind Mark's shoulder, and I glanced in horror at Cupid's eyes. Not only were they midnight blue, but the brightness of his green irises made him look supernatural. What made it worse wasn't the heavy breathing; it wasn't watching Cupid tense his jawline.

But the single, dark blue tear that poured from his left eye, like pen ink, and stained his white shirt. I realized then that Mark wasn't playing a Russian newscast, but a Ukrainian one. It wasn't my blood in the machine; it was Cupid's.

In an instant, Cupid grabbed Mark's neck and threw him onto the grass. People around him scattered as Cupid grabbed the cube speaker, launching it onto the concrete. I knew Cupid wasn't satisfied, and catching my breath, and in a raspy voice, I failed to stop him. Cupid turned around and grabbed the glass bottle from the ground before launching it directly at Mark's head. The sound of the bottle against Mark's skull sent chills down my entire body, and I didn't know if the bottle was Pallet glass or not. I didn't hear it shatter. Mark was unconscious, and I watched Cupid panting over Mark. His white shirt splattered in the blue colored stress fluid, Cupid was crying and shaking, screaming in Slovak.

"He's fucking DEAD. HE is FUCKING GONE!"

His voice was deeper than usual, more grounded. Everybody around him was silent and motionless, and the sounds of the city were the only thing in the soundscape. Cupid ran down the hill at lightning speed, leaving Hampton and me to chase after him. But Cupid was fast, and Hampton was on something that inhibited his athleticism. We lost him as soon as we reached Harlequin campus, the sound of the water from the jester's hand filling the space as Hampton and I panted.

"He's so dramatic," Hampton said, collapsing on a golden bench.

I looked at him in disbelief. "He just cried… blue… you have… no idea what happened to him, do you?"

"Oh, what, he heard… some Slavic whatever and freaked out."

It dawned on me that Hampton was nothing close to Angel in terms of friendship, and that he probably didn't know about what happened a month ago. The cold air dried my lips as I spoke. "It was the same… you know what, forget it. Just because you're suddenly immune to stress doesn't mean…"

"Oh, give me a break. I know his parents are dead, but… I'm not doing this." Hampton threw up his hands, walking toward the Glacier. "I don't want another lecture, TA Teddy," he snarked and walked away.

He was muttering to himself, probably some comeback that he wished he could have said. I didn't have an excuse to dislike Hampton up until now; he was always nice and polite with me. Yet, now I saw him like Cupid did—bitter, selfish, and shallow.

Chapter Eleven

When I got into Cupid's apartment, which was unlocked, Burka rubbed up against my legs as my eyes darted around the room. There was no sign of Cupid's fury; all the artwork intact, crystal untouched, the chairs standing. I walked into his bedroom, clothing everywhere, but relatively how I remembered it, except for one detail. The only thing glaringly different was his center desk drawer, ripped from the desk and upside down on his bed. It was in thinking about Cupid's childhood temper that I knew where to go, after searching on my phone on his couch. After walking twenty minutes, I stood outside the old-looking building before entering. The man behind the counter nodded at me, and an American flag was behind him. He was reading some sort of magazine with an elk on the cover, chewing peanuts from a jar.

"I'm looking for somebody, sir. Um… he's…" In my panic, I stammered while trying to describe Cupid.

"He's in there. The one with…" The worker motioned his hair dramatically, and I nodded.

"Yeah, the hair," I confirmed.

"Got it, yeah. The boy with the pen explosion too. Quite colorful…. uh… He's uh…" The worker, who spoke more slowly once he knew I had an accent, looked at a computer. "He's on Lane Six."

I opened the door and heard gunshots, my nervous system firing before soothing to see Cupid. I hated the sound of gunshots and refused to go hunting with Cupid's dad and my father because of it. My wet sneakers squeaking on the concrete floor in the shooting gallery caused a pair of men to turn to me. I nodded at them before watching Cupid. He stood in perfect formation, like his father taught him, holding a ruby-studded pistol and still wearing the crop top with blue drops on it. His glittering fingernails bear clawing the gun as it remained perfectly still with every pull of the trigger. I stood in Lane Five, able to see both his focused face and target. Shot after shot, Cupid was no longer shooting at the heart of the silhouetted man on the paper, since there was a baseball-sized hole already there. He was shooting in a perfect line across the neck, and once his clip finished, he slammed down the gun. The men next to us clapped at him, complimenting him. Cupid didn't turn, didn't acknowledge them, didn't even want the attention. He just stared forward, his chest rising and falling.

"I kept imagining him on that fucking paper," Cupid said, taking out the clip.

"I know. Mark's an asshole," I whispered.

"No, no, not Mark. Not that little bitch, no."

He shook his head as he pressed the conveyor button, the paper approaching him on the line. I knew who he was talking about now, which made sense why he was here. Since Cupid's father was a welder on the production floor, he would bring home various ammunition for Cupid to try. After he turned ten, various boxes of ammo and guns were the only gifts I saw Cupid get from his father. It was the one thing they could bond over, the one thing they had in common. I marveled at the shiny, studded pistol as he spoke, the glimmers and glints from the harsh light above.

"You know… it makes perfect sense. My family would be the thing that stresses me… no, him. He would be the one who stresses me. I just felt so… sick and nauseous, and angry." Cupid tore the paper and quickly replaced it, sending it far back into the lane for another round. He turned to me; his eyes reddened, and his face tired.

"The fucking thing is… I got into Taupe. It was my top school. And, you know what he said to me?" The door slammed behind us, and I realized the guys had left, leaving

Cupid and me. He reloaded the gun while shaking his head, scoffing before getting his aim ready.

"My father said mental health isn't real. It's a fake field, and I'd be better off putting my personality to use." Cupid then fired multiple shots, piercing a small heart shape into the black paper. The shots echoed through the empty range long after he stopped firing. He continued.

"And... hearing Ukrainian like that. It brought me back to him. Slovak doesn't do that, nor do Polish or Czech. Hell, my body even knows the difference between Russian. But... that... fucking language. I had to train myself to stop... using it in my head. It's the language that I'm the harshest in, the cruelest." He sniffled and wiped his eyes.

While I couldn't discern the difference that sensitively, I knew that Cupid could. I could hear differences in Polish, Slovak, and Czech, but the Cyrillic languages took effort for me, which made sense as to why my body thought it was Russian. Cupid's family was split, half Slovak and half Ukrainian, with his father's side having cousins, aunts, and more complicated dynamics. There were times when we spoke that Cupid would have to repeat himself, slipping into Ukrainian vocab I didn't know. But growing up, I would watch him get scolded by his father in a harsher language, and it all made sense now.

"It's his voice in your head, isn't it. Talking down on you," I said softly.

Cupid turned to me, his lips pressed, nodding. He dropped his head then and started to cry. As I hugged him, I thought about what his father was like, remembering one story specifically. It was his birthday party, he was around seven, at his house, and I remember Cupid, me, and his other cousins were playing soccer. His cousin, Arty, was extremely fast and could do an incredible number of soccer tricks. I wasn't nearly as good, but I could run fairly fast. When Cupid's father called out to us in Ukrainian, Cupid and I stayed behind to kick the ball around. When he stormed down from the porch, he berated Cupid on how much the cake cost, how much he should like it, and how he was taking off work to be here.

"Stefan, absolutely not!" My mother descended the steps, licking icing from the side of her hand and pointing with the other. "You are not going to speak to my son, or yours, in that way. He is turning seven, and you will let him play outside. And, Jesus, it's twenty degrees in February, let them enjoy it, they can come inside when they're ready." My eyes sparkled at my mother as she turned to me. I will never forget when she winked at me, a little "I have your back if anybody comes for you." Cupid's father threw up his hands, and my mother crouched to the crying Cupid.

"Listen. He's just mad because it's not his birthday, and his cake isn't as nice. And…" My mother showed the side of her hand, revealing pink frosting. "I made sure to write your name in your favorite color." A giddy smile came over his face, and my mom lifted him on her shoulders while she held my hand.

"Here comes the birthday prince!" she pronounced, entering the kitchen while Avana planted a kiss on the giddy Cupid.

My mother removed her white flat shoes at the door before crouching down and singing "Happy Birthday" with the others. As for presents, Cupid got a video game console from his parents, a game for that console from one of his aunts, a sweater from another relative, and he got to our box. My mother wrapped it in thin paper, which Cupid tore through quickly. He flipped over the box, and his eyes widened. Cupid's small hands held a pink and black puffer jacket, and he tried it on. He walked immediately to me and hugged me, swinging me in appreciation. I guess my mother said the gift was from me, which I told Cupid my mom helped wrap and pick out.

Later that night, my mother was straining potatoes and talking to my father, who was setting the table. It was one of those conversations that seemed random, but I remembered it so clearly. She called Cupid's father something as she recounted to my father, and told me I could never repeat the word she called him because it was not nice. I kicked my feet as my father placed a spoon in front of me, patting my head and calling me his rascal.

"But… you got him a girl's jacket…" my father said with a sigh.

"And? He likes pink, let him like pink." My mother threw off the oven mitts onto the wooden counter.

"He should be—"

"No." She didn't let him finish. "I am not doing that, not at all. He's seven. He is way too young to expect anything from him."

"Besides…" my mother let out a grunt after pounding potatoes, "I doubt his father will let him wear it out of the house. Your sister, sure. But… I don't know Gregor. He's very cruel."

My father shrugged. "He's Ukrainian… and his family had the war and…"

"I am not going to absolve him of that… he should not talk to children like that, regardless of what he's seen. You've seen things, I've seen things."

"You're so…" my father muttered, smoothing the napkins into neat triangles.

My mother dropped the bowl of potatoes on the table while eyeing my father. "So what?"

"You're so Americanized sometimes."

My mother shook her head, and she sat down quietly. My father cut my steak into cubes, while she dolloped her silky potatoes on my plate. That sort of conversation would normally be forgotten, but it was one of the only dinners I had as a kid in total silence.

#

It was Sunday, and the cold morning air made my face tighten. I got the earliest train back to Hartford, hugging Cupid at the train station. The rest of the night was spent walking back to his apartment and sleeping. Now, I needed time alone and to think, to regroup. I hadn't heard anything about Mark, and people were now calling Cupid the Peppermint Puncher online. Comments from Harlequin students, likes and shares from Taupe students, all dopamine magnets that would drain me further. I deleted the app altogether, which was almost sacrilegious at Taupe. It's how everybody stayed connected and communicated, even professors like Dr. Ilt.

Walking on campus, I stood in front of Khill, and heaved a breath. I stared at the angels and saints that looked down on me, that judged me. I imagined that my parents were doing that, too. My father was probably saying to smile through it, while I imagined my mother saying to write to Dr. Ilt immediately to do damage control and apologize. Yet, thinking about them, I couldn't cry. I was so bored with crying, with yearning for them. In my mind, I felt a hand on my left shoulder. In reality, Angel was standing right next to me, her sclera being a pastel blue.

"Hey, Dr. Teddy," she said softly.

I didn't say a word, I just hugged her. My face pressed against her curls, and I inhaled her apple shampoo as I finally cried. I cried remembering how it was hugging her at the funeral, how it was when she brought me food, how it was all the other times Angel emotionally grounded me. Through the exams I swore I failed, or the times where my mother put pressure on me, or the times I felt homesick, I pulled away and gazed into her dark brown eyes.

"I'm sorry about… snapping at you. You didn't need that. I've been thinking about it a lot," Angel said, wiping a tear from my face with her cold thumb.

"I'm sorry for… being so distant. I was at Harlequin with Cupid and… it was a shit show. Mark showed up and…"

"I was going to ask, how was…"

"Horrible. It's all… horrible. This entire school is fucked, the program is fucked, the Pallet family is… horrible."

A gust of wind produced the sound of flowing fabric behind us, which caused me to turn. Standing behind us like the grim reaper, Dr. Ilt cleared her throat. In a flowing black coat and black sunglasses, she stood by herself, interrupting the moment of tenderness between Angel and me.

"Follow me," was all she said, before turning and walking slowly, her heels clacking in a consistent rhythm.

As I nodded to Angel that it was okay, I didn't know what to expect. Outside the Immunology Building, Dr. Ilt ascended the steps while I turned to my right. It was Mark, his head bandaged, crying with a red envelope in his hands, and two other people whom I quickly named just by looking at them. Mark looked like a younger, thinner version of his father. The man sat on the bench, using hand gestures similar to Mark as he spoke. I could tell that it was philosophical, that Mark's father was trying to convey a point to make Mark feel better. His mother, with her blond bob and pointed nose, nodded to what her husband said. I wasn't close enough to hear them, and didn't want to be. Mark's head rested on his mother's shoulder, and his scrunched face quivered as a hand rubbed his back. Seeing this interaction, which was something I would never have again, led me to stop. And with that realization, my eyes started to make tears of envy, tears of rage. I told Dr. Ilt I would be there in fifteen minutes, saying I needed to drop off my things in my dorm room.

I flung the switch in the room and darted toward the back of the room. I threw the memory box that rested on my desk across the room, leading to an ugly crash from the DVDs, frames, photos, and other fragile things from home, now broken. I felt lost. I was doing this all for them, my parents. I grabbed the box Cupid handed me and pulled out a cigarette. In my trembling hands, I fumbled a cigarette between two fingers. It was one way my mom and I connected in my adulthood. We would sit and smoke, recognizing the irony of our expertise and the damage we were causing to our bodies. Sometimes, our father would join us with a beer, but would never touch a cigarette. Yet, they smelled like home to me.

Balancing it in my lips, I carefully opened the box of memories to reveal envelopes of photos, some in frames. Framed photos of my mother in medical school, at her graduation, photos of my father in the military, and photos of them on various dates in the Slovak countryside. There were trinkets, some documents, but I was searching for something specific. Pushing past frames, plates, and various trinkets made of crystal, I found a case of DVDs. I didn't want to just see my mother, I wanted to hear her, to watch her, to experience her again. Wiping tears that began to fall from my eyes, I set aside three DVDs. I knew that these would be nostalgic since all recent videos were recorded on a video camera. Yet, I decided to watch the videos in reverse chronological order. I started with a DVD that I almost thought of calling Cupid, but didn't. I knew he would be in it, given the title on the disk.

It was my sixth birthday party. My mother was significantly younger and wore a flour-covered apron, frosting cupcakes for what looked like fifty people. She was pointing to Avana, ordering her to turn off the oven. My father zoomed the camera on her smile, the one I shared, before attempting to zoom the camera on her denim-covered rear. I remembered the old kitchen, with the birch cabinets and various pig-themed items. The pine trees in the backyard making my house a fortress. When my mother caught on that the camera was pointed down and began to call out my father, I interrupted him. The camera pointed down at me, my father exclaimed happily, and asked me how old I was turning, who I was excited to see, and what the theme was. Seeing myself as a kid, I slammed the space bar and started to cry. The huge, thick black glasses, the spiky brunette hair, the puffy blue sweater. I was so innocent and pure, coming off of sickness, way before expectations were set. Back then, I just learned what the immune system was, and now I was expected to save the world.

As the video progressed, it was clear that this was before my family had a lot of money. My mother was recording now, and I watched my father and his brother-in-law wheel a large wooden table into the backyard. Little Cupid was behind his father, telling him that he could help. His white shoes and face were dirty, and when my mother called to him, he ran toward her, hugging her leg. This revealed where I was, practically attached to my mom's right leg.

The footage rippled before revealing a slew of people wishing me happy birthday. I stood on a chair with my parents behind me, with a shy but polite smile. Cousins from Cupid's side stood in a line by the table, and one of his aunts was holding a baby who must have been no older than one. Likely Peter, with his sister in front of the woman's legs. When I blew out the candles, I paused the video. The cheap plastic tablecloth, the single birthday candle, the paper hats. The house behind it, which even though it existed, would hurt too much to visit. I knew it would look different now; the panels, a light brown, would soon be a dark gray when we remodeled during my high school years. I ejected the disk and got up. With another cigarette, I brewed a fresh pot of coffee. At one point, there was a knock on my door. It could have been Angel or anybody, yet I had no energy to have another emotional event. I needed to seclude myself.

The next DVD was in a white envelope, with a blue marker spelling out *SVADBA*. I inhaled and clicked the icon on my computer. The video was about thirty minutes long, with the opening shot revealing a church in the center of Košice. People gawked as they walked by, and an old woman in a thick coat waved to the camera. The camera cut into the inside of the church, where blue ribbons and white flowers decorated the aisle. Men in gray suits stood at the altar, with the next shot zooming in on the only man in a black tuxedo.

My father, looking eerily similar to me, smiled with a thick mustache. I slouched on the carpeted floor, my laptop on the ground, as I watched my mother walk down the aisle. Her frame was even more slender, her face youthful and with light, effortless makeup. Her flowing light blond hair dancing down her spine complemented the lace on her back; she looked stunning. At the altar, Cupid's mom had way too much makeup and wiped a mascara-running tear with her blue dress. The next shot was my parents' first dance, where my father and mother looked at each other lovingly. It reminded me of how Angel looked at Paul, the devotion in their eyes. During the reception, I could see Avana singing on the stage, singing some American pop songs. Behind her, a man with medium-length black hair bobbed his head to the rhythm, playing a guitar with black fingernails. I twisted my head and slammed the space bar, only to register that it was Cupid's father. I knew that his mother used to sing, but the fact that his father was in her band complicated his image even further. The next shot was my mother sitting down, holding the hand of one of her bridesmaids. The cameraman walked toward her, but my mother shooed him away. From what I could see, she was wrapping gauze around the girl's hand. The frame quickly went to my parents slow dancing, before another knock was at my door. I ignored it before I heard someone talking, and then the sound of my door opening. I jumped up, slamming the lights on and throwing my cigarette into my coffee cup.

A voice from behind the bedroom door called, before I realized who it was. "Teddy?"

I ruffled my hair slightly before opening the door, revealing Dr. Ilt. She scanned my room before entering.

"You know that smoking is…"

"Yeah. I know it is, I'm sorry. Just… I was triggered by… something today."

"Hm." Dr. Ilt walked around my room, looking at the mess and the box ripped open. She walked around to my depression circle on the ground, the cup of coffee, the cigarette box, another mug for ashes, and my cell phone.

"This is a… cute setup," she said, indifferently.

"Thanks."

Dr. Ilt crouched down and hit the space bar, watching my parents dance with her head tilted.

"Your parents?"

"Yeah. Those are my parents, I'm watching their wedding footage."

"Hm. A long time ago…"

I grew suspicious and impatient, especially given how calm she was. "Why are you here?"

"Well… you didn't respond to my Portal message. I looked up your room and asked your RA."

Angel. She was let in by Angel. It was ironic, but it must have been important since I had never seen a professor near a dorm hall. It also felt invasive, the way she looked at my laptop and my room. My hair was undone, and the smell of cigarettes no longer reminded me of mornings at home, but I felt the embarrassment of vulnerability.

"I saw you storm past Mark's parents. Lovely people, by the way. I had the chance to talk to them before visiting you. But I wanted to check in."

"I'm fine… is that all?"

She blinked at me, like I was starving, and slapped her hand away. The height difference was prominent; even with her wearing sneakers, she was taller than me.

"Well… fine. Just wanted to make sure that you were fine. Come to my office for…"

"For another test? A humiliation ritual?" I snapped. She tilted her head, offended by my tone.

"For your offer, Teddy. The Pallets are coming tomorrow, but... it was ultimately my decision. You were my first choice, frankly, this entire time. But I want to explain something to you." Because Dr. Ilt spoke Czech, there was a better understanding, and I could read her face. After I was finished voicing how I felt, I stood still as she went to the box in the corner silently, stepping over paper DVD sleeves.

"No! Don't touch those, that's personal."

She revealed my mother's medical school diploma, before shattering it with her knuckle and dumping the glass in the box. I moved toward her, only to be halted by her hand. After shaking the snow-looking glass specs into the sunset-lit box, she carefully slid her finger on the paper. She smirked as, in front of my eyes, my jaw dropped as she peeled the paper back. She plucked the diploma with "Angelika Dolakova" plastered in thick ink, before shredding it loudly in front of me.

"No!" I rushed to Dr. Ilt, fighting the urge to slap her hand.

"Look." She dropped the diploma frame, which now rested on my desk. The frame had another diploma staring back at me.

My mother's name, the exact same degree, but now in Latin writing. The only difference was the school, which now printed "Cardinal University of Medicine" at the top. As I processed slowly and the hints from childhood came together, I looked up. When Dr. Ilt held the laptop, she paused on my mother wrapping the gauze. Dr. Ilt's lips pressed together, as I saw the video paused on the bridesmaid with gauze hands. Dr. Ilt held up her hand, revealing a deep gash alongside the palm.

"It was a broken wine glass, your aunt knocked it over, and I tried to pick it up. You want me to explain now?"

#

"Lock the door," she commanded directly. Her office seemed bare now, almost sterile with its purple and black decorations. Still, it was the same orchids, the same photos, and the same glass sculptures. Going to the door, I heard glass clinking behind me as she grabbed two champagne flutes.

"How. How did you know my mother?" I had a million questions, and could only say that one.

"We roomed together. But, when everything happened… well, it doesn't matter. You made it. Angel's son… going to be a doctor now."

In a moment that should have felt earned, rewarding, and amazing, I felt dirty. I felt wrong, and it felt inappropriate. My mind was swirling with the lies my mother said about her collegiate experience in Slovakia, or was Dr. Ilt lying? The certainty that she cracked the diploma, which sat in the box the entire time, I felt myself drowning in my own logic. Now, I almost didn't want to accept the position.

"What's going to happen to Mark?"
"They might nail him for cheating or something, sure. But…" She plucked a red thread from her sweater with her fingers. "I can tell you, he's not going to be here next semester." A chill ran down my spine. I sat across from her, twisting the thread on the inside of my cuff that I embroidered two years ago.

"So, then, if I may ask, why did you pick me? But also…forgive me for asking…why didn't they expel me if they knew about my virus? The one that didn't work?"

I knew the question sounded insecure, but I was already vulnerable. And, if Dr. Ilt wanted me gone, I rationalized, she could do so quickly. She could lie to the Pallets with some scientific reason they didn't understand, and move on. I would be seen as I always was: another number, a failed product, another student dismissed for reasons not investigated.

"Your virus worked, just on other people. You were always smarter, and you always had my vote. But the Pallets wanted to eliminate any bias from my decision, so they decided to put you both to the test when you both made viruses. I thought it was a horrible idea, which is why I told Peter only about you."

"So… you…"

"I knew that it was a matter of time before Mark cracked, that he would say something or do something. And well…" Dr. Ilt unwrapped a candy from a glass bowl, a peppermint that she popped into her mouth. "He certainly put on a show."

"You knew about it? When did he make it?"

"Two days after you made yours. You both did the same haphazard clicking, the same sloppy roll of the genetic dice. ILLUMAKE, at that level, isn't going to give you what you want. You have to code it in great detail, and well… you both got somewhat lucky."

I got a headache, half fueled by guilt, as Dr. Ilt continued, "But, Milena and Hawley were impressed by your poise. Your… silent demeanor and confidence. To them, you seemed perfect for their mission of having brilliant problem solvers. No… not problem solvers… problem identifiers. Not problem makers, either. You don't want to actually solve the problem, but you can profit from it. They don't want… another Cardinal." She paused and poured a drink. Her wedding ring was sparkling in the overhead light. "Cardinal produced too many smart doctors, like your mother, you see, too many educated people, too many… problem solvers. You cure everybody, and… well… there's no money in that. Instead, you want students… people who can obey… whether or not they want to. To cure what they want you to cure. Who is going to work for the Pallets when they see the system as a whole? And Cardinal produced so many doctors at once… albeit mean doctors, cutthroat doctors, that… they needed to shut it down."

Dr. Ilt's email rang from her computer, and she gave an affirming nod.

"And well, I told the Pallets to keep you both. It would look odd if they expelled both of you, so I convinced them to see what would happen. In my opinion, you went for self-preservation, you... defended yourself against the environment. Mark did the opposite. I thought it was... telling how you made your stress eating virus, for other people, of course. Although in the program, you will learn how to actually make a cortisol-eating virus, one that works the way you want. But..." Her phone buzzed, and she checked the clock and not her phone at all.

"Check your phone," she asked quietly. When I did, there was nothing different. It wasn't until I was instructed to redownload the Pallet Portal and refresh it once more that my jaw dropped.

EVIDENCE TIES MARK DRYKOVCZYNSKI TO BEV VIRUS, CHESHIRE-YU LAB SUGGESTS.

Suddenly, I felt the mental smog of guilt, of keeping secrets, vanish. I had nothing to hide, and realized that I had some power now over the Pallets and Dr. Ilt.

"I accept the cohort spot under one condition," I stated, bluntly.

"Oh? And... What is that condition? I can't—"

"You will guarantee," I ordered. I was no longer being defensive or playing the victim. Now, I felt intoxicated by the leverage I had. Dr. Ilt scoffed at my boldness before gesturing to me to continue.

"I want my cousin and Angel Marsa to have guaranteed acceptance into any PharmD lab of their choosing. I get to be in the doctoral cohort if they get to be in another cohort. Which one... that's up to them."

Dr. Ilt puffed a sigh before staring out her glass window. "I'll see what I can do."

Epilogue

The blizzard outside coated the pine trees and the entire campus, making Khill barely visible from my bedroom. When Angel knocked, I told her that she could key in. Angel walked in with two bags for Cupid and me, along with a bottle with a green bow on it.

"You ever had horchata?"

"What?"

"It's… never mind, just try it."

Angel grabbed a mug from my coffee machine and poured the liquid inside. When I tasted it, I told her how good it would be with coffee; the sweet and cinnamon flavor would go extremely well with it.

"Do you want to open it now or… when Cupid gets here?"

"We can wait," I said, handing her the box. "Let me see where he is."

I climbed onto my bed, and below the painting Cupid had gotten me for my newly decorated room. I banged on the wall. We invented this system to communicate, and since we were in the corner rooms, nobody else would hear. Across the wall, I could hear him tell me he was coming, and shortly after, he banged on my front door.

"Merry Christmas, losers! I brought gifts!" Cupid hugged both of us and went to the common area.

"Ugh, and look at this tree!" In his puffy sweater, he theatrically opened his arms.

"You bought it… and decorated it," I remarked

"No, I know. But… it looks so good. It's so you."

It was about the height of Cupid, with Pallet glass ornaments shaped in various birds. Silver tinsel and white lights gave the room a beautiful, sparkling glow. Cupid and Angel opened each other's first, as I sipped my horchata. Cupid got Angel a designer handbag, which she almost refused to accept, whereas Angel got Cupid an eyeshadow palette.

"Now… my gift is a little different," I admitted.

I handed them both envelopes, the exact same paper. My heart raced as I watched them open it. I had to sit down with all the Pallet siblings and watch each one of them, with my lawyer, sign the document. It was an agreement that both Cupid and Angel would have a guaranteed spot in the neurology cohort of their choosing. It would be completely funded, with living expenses also included in a luxury apartment in Hartford.

I watched Angel's face drop, and Cupid reread the document several times. They didn't need to know that I patented my stress cure and that I signed away the rights to the Pallets. That, from here on out, I no longer could produce, code, or have anything to do with my stress cure. That I could no longer use cortisol or anything cortisol-related in my future pharmaceutical studies. Cupid and Angel didn't need to know that. Like them, I would be entering a doctoral cohort from ground zero.

The Author

J.M. Netopier is a novelist, entrepreneur, lecturer, and designer who values authentic expression in all creative forms. Born in Connecticut, Netopier's upbringing was heavily influenced by the medical industry and Slavic culture. With a Master's in Public Health from Brown University, Netopier's work blends concepts of epidemiology, queer culture, and speculative fiction into multi-layered universes. In his spare time, J.M. Netopier likes to design clothing, run, and drink his weight in coffee. He currently resides in Providence, Rhode Island, with his cat, Myszka.

www.ingramcontent.com/pod-product-compliance
Lightning Source LLC
Chambersburg PA
CBHW070003180726
48002CB00019B/1890